## "You're very easy to read."

"You don't say." Joel slouched back in his chair and stared at Melissa. "So read me."

She stared at him for a moment. "You have a deep-seated desire to be independent, free from all restraints and routines. You're easily bored and need to be constantly stimulated."

Alarms rang inside Joel's head. He'd felt the same way when he'd read that absurd piece about the Gemini man in the Sunday paper. He resented the fact that she had been able to describe him so accurately.

"What are you, some kind of witch?"

"Was I close?"

"Close enough."

"Now you do me," she invited.

He was quiet for a moment. Then in a low voice, he began. "You have eyes that haunt my sleep and a mouth that continues to lure me into indiscretions that could get me into serious trouble. And you have a very becoming blush that appears at the most intriguing moments . . . such as now."

Dear Reader,

June is traditionally the month of weddings, and at Silhouette Romance, wedding bells are definitely ringing! Our heroines this month will fulfill their hearts' desires with the kinds of heroes you've always dreamed of—from the dark, mysterious stranger to the lovable boy-next-door. Silhouette Romance novels *always* reflect the magic of love—sweeping you away with heartwarming, poignant stories that will move you time and time again.

In the next few months, we'll be publishing romances by many of your all-time favorites, including Diana Palmer, Brittany Young and Annette Broadrick. And, as promised, Nora Roberts begins her CALHOUN WOMEN series this month with the Silhouette Romance, *Courting Catherine*.

WRITTEN IN THE STARS is a very special event for 1991. Each month, we're proud to present a Silhouette Romance that focuses on the hero—and his astrological sign. June features one of the most enigmatic, challenging men of all—*The Gemini Man*. Our authors and editors have created this delightfully romantic series especially for you, the reader, and we'd love to hear what you think. After all, at Silhouette Romance, we take our readers' comments to heart!

Please write to us at Silhouette Romance
　　　　　　　　　　300 East 42nd Street
　　　　　　　　　　New York, NY 10017

We look forward to hearing from you!

Sincerely,

Valerie Susan Hayward
Senior Editor

# ANNETTE BROADRICK

# The Gemini Man

*Silhouette* *Romance*

Published by Silhouette Books New York

**America's Publisher of Contemporary Romance**

For Jon, another Gemini

**SILHOUETTE BOOKS**
300 E. 42nd St., New York, N.Y. 10017

---

## *ANNETTE BROADRICK*

lives in Missouri on the shores of Lake of the Ozarks, where she spends her time doing what she loves most—reading and writing romance fiction. Since 1984, when her first book was published, Annette has been delighting her readers with her imaginative and innovative style. In addition to being nominated by *Romantic Times* as one of the Best New Authors of that year, she has also won the *Romantic Times* Reviewers' Choice Award for Best in its Series for *Heat of the Night, Mystery Lover* and *Irresistible;* the *Romantic Times* WISH Award for her hero in *Strange Enchantment;* and the *Romantic Times* Lifetime Achievement Award for Series Romance.

## A NOTE FROM THE AUTHOR

Dear Reader,

I chose to write about a Gemini because I find Geminis fascinating people. I have friends and family members who were born between May 21 and June 21 and without exception, I have found them to be multitalented, multifaceted individuals, roguishly charming and infinitely complex.

It cannot be easy to have been born under the sign of the Twins. How does a person decide which personality to bring forth? How does a person placate the energetic and restless nature that pulls in two different directions at once?

It must be a difficult task, but as a writer, I find the Gemini personality eminently fun to explore and develop. I chose a Libra as a counterpoint in order to challenge Gemini's mercurial disposition with a massive dose of logic and superior intellect that won't let him get away with much of anything. Sparks are guaranteed to fly, but, oh! what a lovely display of fireworks for you, the reader.

Enjoy!

Annette Broadrick

# Prologue

"*T*he Gemini man is not a discerning woman's first choice for a mate if she is looking for a stable homelife and steady companion, although his charm and mental agility may cause her to forget all of her dreams if he is determined to sweep her off her feet. However, a wise woman must use caution and look past his seemingly ageless and invariably attractive countenance to what truly motivates a Gemini man: change.

For, you see, the Gemini man truly thrives on challenges; boredom swiftly sets in when he finds himself confined to a routine of any kind. His ruling planet is Mercury, the planet that controls communications of all kinds, and his mercurial temperament is readily apparent to all who attempt to draw close to him. *Attempt* is the operative term because our Gemini man does not want anyone to know who he truly is. In fact, he isn't all that certain, himself. It is no coincidence that the astrological sign for Gemini is the Twins. You see, our exhil-

*arating charmer has a dual personality in many respects.
He changes his style of dress, his work, his residence,
and, yes, my dear, even his love interest, with alarming
ease and regularity. He looks for excitement and constant
challenge and is determined to disguise his true feelings
and desires from those around him.*

*However, his high energy, his focused interest and
charming friendliness sometimes encourages a courageous soul to abandon her caution in an effort to draw
closer and attempt to better understand our quicksilver,
chameleonlike friend. We may curse him all the while we
pursue him, knowing that his mental agility will never
allow him to be caught—unless he wants to be, of course.
And that, dear friends, is the hope that keeps those who
love a Gemini man in determined pursuit. If he chooses
to share his life with you, make sure that you don't allow yourself to become entrapped in dull routine and
drudgery. Become a part of his life if you insist, but only
at the risk of your need for stability at home.''*

Joel Kramer stared blindly at the pages spread before
him, feeling conspicuous and exposed, even though he
was alone in his small apartment. The astrological profile had fallen from one of the Sunday supplements of the
paper, carefully categorizing both sexes of each of the
twelve astrological signs. Because he'd had nothing better to do, he had decided to read what had been written,
even though he didn't believe in that sort of thing.

The precision with which he had been portrayed had
more than surprised him. He'd had a shock that made
him wince. He didn't like the flippant summary of his
personality or the comments regarding his basic characteristics. Joel didn't like the idea that he could be so accurately described. He had a real aversion toward anyone

knowing him quite so well. Exactly what the article had said.

Damn! He tossed the offending paper aside and stood, ramming his hands into his pants pockets. He began to pace.

Max had promised to get back to him. Max knew him as well as, if not better than, any other person in the world. He knew that Joel detested inactivity. Once again he winced, remembering the article. Yes, Joel avoided any sort of occupation that was filled with monotonous routine.

He walked to the window and looked down at the river that wound through the wintry Virginia landscape below. It looked cold and forbidding, accurately reflecting what he was feeling at the moment.

At times like this, Joel questioned the wisdom of replacing his father on the agency's payroll. He'd grown up with a parent who had rarely been at home and he'd learned to resent the occupation that had robbed him of a father. But it had taken only one assignment to hook Joel. He'd quickly become addicted to the danger, the uncertainty, the variety of what the agency called on him to do. His first assignment had been twelve years ago. The irony of agreeing to step in and fulfill his father's last assignment had never left him.

Max encouraged Joel's talent for doing the unexpected, for ferreting out information that no one else seemed to find. And yet, for all that, Joel didn't know which branch of the intelligence service he worked for. All he knew was that Max was his only contact with the government.

Joel was good at what he did. He took a certain amount of pride in that knowledge.

Exactly what did he do? Once again he frowned at the offending page that lay scattered in front of his easy chair. Yes. He lead a double life. He was in fact two people—as much as was physically possible for one person without being labeled schizophrenic. His neighbors thought of him as a quiet man who lived alone, who was gone for long periods of time. The landlord had no complaints, either about Joel or from him. He paid his rent on time. He left others alone.

When Max needed him, Joel became whatever Max needed. He gathered information; he watched other people. Like a chameleon, he blended into his surroundings.

Why?

Because he enjoyed the challenge. Because he thrived on outwitting his enemies, staying one step ahead of them in their mental gymnastics.

A mercurial temperament, indeed!

The phone interrupted his frustrated comparisons between his personality and the one described for all the world to see. He felt relief flow through him at the interruption. He knew it was Max before he answered the phone. Who else ever called him? There were no close ties in his life. He didn't need them. He couldn't afford them.

"Yes?"

"You sound a little frustrated, Kramer. Ready to go to work?"

"You know damn well I am."

"I'm afraid the only thing I've got on the books at the moment is a little out of your line. If you don't want to take it, I'll understand."

"At the moment, I'm in no mood to quibble."

"I have a situation that could escalate into a crisis at any time. In order to brief you properly, I need you to meet me. There's someone you'll need to talk with for the necessary background." He gave Joel the name of a hospital and a room number. Joel happened to know that very few people knew of the existence of that particular facility. It was used only for the highest security cases.

"I'll be there."

Joel felt the adrenaline pumping in his bloodstream as he hung up the phone. By the time he left his apartment, the astrology profile had been dismissed from his mind.

Joel went through extensive screening at four separate checkpoints before he made it to the floor where he was to meet Max. This was the first time he'd walked into the place. The only other time he'd been there he'd been brought in unconscious. He'd been a terrible patient. The memories of those days when he'd been so helpless, when he had been forced to rely on others to care for him, flooded his mind at the sights, sounds and smells that surrounded him.

He shrugged his shoulders as though he could shift the memories back where they belonged. As he approached the door to the designated room, Max stepped out and nodded in recognition. "Thanks for your promptness," he said, offering his hand in greeting.

Joel grasped the hand and shook it. "No problem. What's going on?" He glanced around.

"We're not sure, but we don't like the feel of this one. I don't believe in coincidences, and this one is a little too convenient." He motioned Joel around the corner to a grouping of chairs. They sat facing each other. Max leaned back in his chair before continuing.

"Dr. Peter Feldman is one of the foremost research scientists in the United States. Although he is on the payroll of a private corporation, the government has followed his research with a good deal of interest. What he's working on has a great deal of bearing on what we're battling on the domestic front at the moment."

Joel forced himself to assume a relaxed position, sitting back in the chair and placing his elbows on the arm rests.

Max went on. "The war against drugs must be won in this country if we are to survive. However, as long as there is a demand, there will be those countries and people who will supply what is wanted." He paused, raising his eyebrows slightly, as though to invite comment. Joel said nothing since many of his overseas assignments had been gathering information that supported Max's statements.

After a moment, Max continued. "What Dr. Feldman has been working on so diligently is a drug that we hope will be a breakthrough in the field of withdrawal from chemical dependency—such as alcohol and drug addiction." He leaned forward. "He's on the trail of what may prove to be an antidote that, when taken, will cause the body to no longer crave the effects of the particular substance that caused the addiction."

Joel abandoned his casual pose. He leaned forward and asked, "Do you mean a drug to be taken in place of more harmfully addictive drugs?"

"Hopefully the body will eventually develop its own immunity to the abused substances. What Dr. Feldman is currently working on is a short-term regimen that not only will detoxify the body, but help it to overcome the cravings of the particular addiction. The end result, hopefully, will be a permanent repugnance to all types of mood-altering drugs."

Joel whistled softly. "Use of such a drug would effectively demolish the drug trade as we know it."

"Exactly."

"You think somebody knows what Dr. Feldman's been working on?"

"Had you asked that a few hours ago, I would have been emphatic in denying the idea. This particular research project has been as closely guarded as the development of the atom bomb."

"So what happened today?"

"Dr. Feldman decided to go into the lab yesterday, even though it was a Saturday, to catch up on some of the paperwork. He was on his way home last night when his car was run off the road as it approached an embankment. God only knows how he managed to get out before the car went over. He suffered a broken leg and several severe cuts and bruises. He'd already been briefed on who to contact if he ever felt suspicious of anything that occurred around him. One of the first cars on the scene had a cellular phone. He had the driver call us, and we immediately got help out to him."

"And brought him here."

"Yes."

"Did he see the car that ran him off the road?"

"No. It was already dark by the time he left for home. He was traveling a wooded stretch of roadway. Whoever hit him had come up on him without lights. The impact was the first he knew something was wrong."

"You want me to investigate this matter?" Joel asked, his mind already reviewing and arranging the information Max had given him.

"No. What I have in mind is not quite so straightforward. We already have people working on the accident and its causes. What Dr. Feldman is concerned about is his assistant. That's where you come in."

Joel frowned slightly. "He thinks his assistant may be behind this?"

Max shook his head. "Not at all. He thinks his assistant might be the next target, if this is, in fact, related to their research."

"Which we don't know at this point, I take it?"

"Like I said, I've never cared for coincidences."

"So where do I fit in?"

Max stood and motioned to the room he'd come out of earlier. "I want you to meet Dr. Feldman. He'll be able to explain his concerns to you."

The two men entered the hospital room. Joel paused just inside the door, fighting the memories. Damn, but he hated hospitals! Max walked over to the bed, and Joel slowly followed.

The man lying there was hooked up to various monitoring machines. His left leg was in a cast and in traction. There were several bandages on his arms, hands and around his head. One side of his face was swollen and discolored.

"Dr. Feldman," Max said, "I'd like you to meet the man I spoke of earlier, Joel Kramer."

Joel stepped closer. A pair of vivid blue eyes stared up at him from the battered face. There was no denying the intelligence in them. "I'm sorry that our meeting came about as a result of your injuries, Dr. Feldman. Max tells me that you are doing some innovative research."

Joel knew that the man on the bed had to be in a great deal of pain. He recognized the lack of a narcotic glaze in the eyes that watched him so intently. They reflected the man's pain as well as his refusal to accept relief. "Thank you for coming," Peter said in a weak voice. "Max assures me that you are one of his most competent men."

Joel glanced at his employer. "I'll remind him of that when my raise comes due."

Max characteristically ignored his jibe and spoke directly to the man in the bed. "Dr. Feldman, perhaps you would like to explain to Joel your concern for Dr. Jordan's safety under the present circumstances."

Dr. Feldman nodded his head slightly. "Yes. She was my first concern when I realized that what happened to me might not be an accident. Max insists that we keep what happened to me quiet. Since I had been planning to take a few days off next week, he wants me to call in sick tomorrow and take the vacation early without letting anyone know the truth, even Dr. Jordan."

"You don't agree?"

"Well, I understand the need for secrecy, but I also don't want to take the chance of having something happen to Dr. Jordan." He closed his eyes for a moment. When he opened them again, Joel could see the pain he fought to ignore. "You see, she isn't aware of the specific nature of our research. I've kept her working on highly specialized tasks without giving her the reasons. I didn't want to place her in a situation where she could be taken advantage of." He moved his head wearily on the pillow. "Over the past several hours, I've come to face the fact that my efforts to protect her were pointless. If someone knows what I am working on, they will automatically assume that my assistant is fully aware of the nature of my research. Her lack of knowledge wouldn't protect her from them." He glanced at Max with an apologetic look. "Even if I tried to warn her, I'm not at all certain that she would believe me. You see, my assistant believes that I have an overactive imagination, which she points out comes from my consuming interest in reading adventure novels." He smiled at the men standing beside his bed. "I must admit that I'm somewhat addicted to them. I read before bedtime as a way to relax in order to sleep. If I explained what happened, she would probably insist that my accident has nothing to do with our research." He moved restlessly in the bed. "And, of course, I can't prove that it has." He focused his gaze on Joel. "But I don't want to take even the slightest chance where she's concerned."

"I see," Joel replied. "I can understand your concern." He glanced at Max. "Don't you trust her to know what is going on?"

"It's not a matter of trust. I want everything to go along as it has without causing possible suspicion in case someone is watching the lab. However, we have already tightened the security, so there is no possibility that anyone could reach her at work."

Joel looked at Max. "Are you suggesting that I need to set up some sort of protective surveillance for Dr. Jordan?"

"Exactly. However, because we don't want to needlessly alarm her, I want you to go in under wraps."

"Protective custody isn't exactly my line of work," Joel pointed out mildly.

"I know," Max agreed. "We can always get someone else to handle this, if you'd like. But since you've been keeping my phone ringing demanding that I give you something to do, I thought you might be willing to take this one."

Joel sighed. As usual, Max knew his people very well. Of course, Joel wasn't going to turn a job down, even if it meant glorified baby-sitting...with a baby who wasn't supposed to know what he was doing!

Max looked at Joel as though waiting for him to deny his comments, but, of course, Joel couldn't. When it became obvious to Max that Joel had nothing further to say, he nodded and said, "The problem as I see it is that Dr. Jordan may or may not be in danger. At this point, we have to assume that she is. Nevertheless, I see no reason to alarm her at this point." He glanced at Joel. "Which is why we prefer that you make yourself a part of her life without her knowing why."

Joel lifted one eyebrow. "In other words, lie to the woman."

"There's no reason to lie. She just doesn't need to know the truth. It so happens that the couple who live directly across from her apartment in Alexandria received a sudden windfall. They are currently closing on the purchase of a condominium near their daughter's home in Florida, which means that their apartment has recently become available."

A fortuitous windfall, indeed, Joel thought cynically.

Max continued. "The apartment is quite nice, and we feel certain that you will be comfortable staying there while you pursue a neighborly acquaintance with Dr. Jordan."

Joel almost groaned aloud. This was not the kind of work he was used to. It wasn't the kind of work he was trained to do. But it was better than sitting at home staring at the four walls. Barely.

"When do I move in?"

Max allowed his features to register surprise. "You mean you'll do it?"

As if there had ever been a doubt in Max's mind! Joel went along with the charade. "Why not? I'm tired of kicking my heels waiting for something to do."

"Your enthusiasm overwhelms me," Max commented.

"I want to make it clear," Dr. Feldman said, "that I don't want Dr. Jordan to feel that she is being spied upon. You see, she is brilliant in the laboratory, her IQ is startling, but she is quite young and inexperienced. I suppose I've become a father figure in her life, in a way. Both of her parents are gone, and she was an only child. I find her modesty refreshing at times, but there are times, such as now, when I recognize that she doesn't realize just how valuable she is to us...or how valuable she would be if the wrong type of people were to get their hands on her."

"Just how young is this woman?" Joel asked.

"Twenty-two."

"Isn't that rather young for the type of work she does?"

"Oh, yes. The woman is truly remarkable. She received her doctorate by the time she was nineteen."

Joel had a mental picture of a studious young woman wearing thick-lensed glasses, a voluminous lab coat and sturdy shoes. She was probably extremely timid, scared of any unexpected sound. And he had to try to befriend her. Great. Just great. He looked at Max. "When do I move in?"

"Tomorrow will be soon enough," Max replied. "Do you know how to type?"

"No. Why?"

"We have to have a reason why you don't leave for work each day. I thought you could tell her that you've taken some time off from your regular job to write a novel."

Joel looked at Max in irritation. "Do I look like a writer to you? Come on, Max. I don't know anything about writing."

Max shrugged. "Doesn't matter. Everyone is convinced that he or she could be a writer if they could find the time to do it. Convince her you're following your dream. Who knows, maybe she can give you some ideas for a story."

Joel shook his head. Sometimes Max's logic eluded him. "You're sure this is the only thing you've got for me to do?"

Max nodded, not bothering to hide his amusement.

"All right, then. Give me the address. I'll go home and pack." Joel glanced down at the man lying on the bed. "In the meantime, you concentrate on getting well. I'll look after your Dr. Jordan."

Dr. Feldman made a slight sound that might have been a chuckle, then winced. He closed his eyes for a moment before speaking. "Oh, she isn't mine, Mr. Kramer. I'm afraid that Melissa Jordan is totally dedicated to her work. She doesn't seem to have any other interests or hobbies. Her work means everything to her."

"Then she and Joel should get along very well," Max said with a glance at Joel. "He shares a similar trait."

Joel frowned, suddenly remembering the astrology article and what it had said. Like it or not, Joel knew that the article had described him to a T. He didn't like having people know that much about him, including the man he worked for.

He glanced at Max. "I'll be in touch." His first priority was to get out of there. He had a definite allergic reaction to the sight and smell of a hospital.

At least he had something to do, even if it was babysitting a success-driven scientist. Max was right. They probably did have a few things in common.

# *Chapter One*

Melissa Jordan pulled into the underground parking garage of her high-rise apartment building with a sense of relief. She couldn't remember having experienced such a chaotic day in her entire career. Unfortunately, the blame could be laid at Dr. Feldman's door.

The poor man. As if he didn't have enough to cope with, he ended up coming down with the flu just a few short days before his vacation. She had offered to go to his home and check on him when he'd called that morning, but he'd insisted that he would be all right with a few days of rest. He'd been very apologetic, but, of course, he couldn't help being ill. She sighed. Regardless of the reason, his absence complicated her job. She would just have to do the best she could and wait for his return in a couple of weeks.

Melissa stepped out of her small, bright red sports car and walked over to the elevator. She shivered, tugging her coat and hood more closely around her. She could feel the gusty wind blowing through the parking area. She glanced around uneasily at the dimly lit garage. What was wrong with her today? She'd never been bothered about coming home alone before. The security of her building was one of the reasons she had moved to her present apartment. The iron-grid gate would only open for a specific code that needed to be punched into the system. Even then, only one car could get through before the gate closed.

She was just tired, that's all.

After punching the button on the elevator, Melissa leaned against the concrete wall and stared down at the toes of her scarlet pumps. Her heavy winter coat ended at her hips, revealing the skirt of her red woolen suit. The cold air seemed to encircle her legs. She shivered again, reminding herself that at least she'd gotten through the day. By tomorrow, there would be some type of organization set up until Dr. Feldman returned.

As soon as the elevator doors opened, she stepped inside and pushed the button for the fifth floor. She removed the fur-trimmed hood of her coat from her head, relieved to be out of the wind, grateful for the relative warmth of the unheated elevator. The first thing she intended to do when she reached her apartment was to take a long, soaking bath. Not only would the hot water warm her chilled body, but it would also help to remove the tension that had her muscles in knots.

When the elevator reached her floor, she stepped out and headed down the hallway, digging for her keys in her purse.

A slight sound startled her, causing her to raise her head with a jerk.

A man stood in front of the door opposite hers, placing a key in the lock. She'd never seen him before. He glanced around at her, giving her a chance to study him.

He was only a few inches taller than she was with her high heels. Candid silver-gray eyes peered at her from behind rimless glasses. He hadn't gotten that deep tan from around here, she decided. His light brown hair had streaks of blond or silver, she couldn't decide which.

He looked away from her and fumbled with his key. This *must be my new neighbor.* Normally, Melissa wouldn't have dreamed of speaking to a man she didn't know. But if he was going to be her neighbor, that was different. Besides, the startled look he'd given her suggested that he might be shy.

"Have you just moved in?" she asked. The sudden sound of her voice in the quiet hall seemed to startle them both.

He turned his head and glanced at her. "Oh, I, uh—yes. I just moved in this morning."

He had trouble meeting her eyes, and she smiled. *Why, he is shy,* she decided. Impulsively, she held out her hand. "I'm Melissa Jordan, your neighbor. There's just these two apartments on this floor."

The man studied her hand as though unsure what he was supposed to do with it. Tentatively touching it with his fingers, he nodded. "Pleased to meet you."

She could have sworn she saw a blush touch his cheeks. Probably not. His tan would camouflage such a betrayal.

She turned away and put her key into her door. When it opened, she gave him a little wave. "If I can be of any help to you, don't hesitate to knock. I know how it is, trying to get settled in."

She closed the door, almost amused at the look of stunned disbelief on the man's face. Maybe he wasn't used to friendly neighbors. Well, he could just get used to it, she decided, kicking off her shoes and shrugging out of her coat.

She missed the elderly couple who had suddenly decided to move to Florida to be closer to their daughter. They were the kind of family she'd never had—warm and friendly, popping over to bring her freshly baked bread and cookies, inviting her to share an occasional meal. They had shown her nothing but kindness. If she could, she'd like to repay that kindness by offering a stranger a friendly smile and a warm hello. Maybe this weekend she'd bake him some cookies or something.

Melissa headed for the bedroom, where she intended to get out of her clothes and enjoy a nice, soaking bath.

Joel stood in the hallway, staring at the door marked 5A. *That* was Melissa Jordan? That was the scientist who needed protecting? Was this some kind of joke that Max had decided to play on him?

Melissa Jordan was a far cry from Joel's imagined laboratory assistant. Even in the bulky coat, he'd recognized that her tall, lithe figure would look right at home walking down the runway of a beauty contest. Wide-spaced blue eyes had stared at him from behind thickly fringed black lashes. A slight dimple had flashed in her right cheek when she'd smiled. Her honey-blond hair had been pulled back from her face in a professional coil at her neck and he'd had the unnerving impulse to pull the pins out of it just to see what she would look like with it tumbling around her shoulders.

Joel had a strict policy of never mixing business with personal pleasure. In the past, that philosophy had never come under scrutiny. But how in the world was he supposed to become platonic friends with a woman whose very presence caused his body to instantly respond to her beauty? Even her voice had started an itch somewhere deep inside of him.

He's spent the day familiarizing himself with the location of the building and its surrounding area, checking the security of the building. He'd been given a description of the car owned by Dr. Jordan so that he'd been aware of her arrival. He'd made certain that he was in the hallway when she stepped off the elevator so that he could casually meet her. What had caught him off guard was how differently she looked from the way he'd imagined her. This was no timid laboratory mouse. Melissa Jordan was a real fox.

He could just hear Max laughing if he tried to complain that the woman he was to protect was too good-looking and would be a distraction in his efforts to do his job. No doubt Max would have him back in the hospital... only this time on the psychiatric floor.

The problem was that a job of this nature was way out of his field of expertise. Was Max deliberately giving him assignments that he considered safe? Didn't he trust Joel to take care of himself after that last fiasco?

Only Max knew what he was thinking, and Joel knew beyond any doubt that Max would only tell him what Max decided he needed to know.

Once again, Joel looked at the door opposite his own. At least the first hurdle had been overcome—Dr. Jordan knew that he was her new neighbor. It was now up to him to make the next move.

Melissa sank into the water-filled tub and let out a sigh of pleasure. Heaven, that's what it was. Pure, unadul-

terated heaven. For a while, she blanked out her
thoughts. Instead, she allowed herself to enjoy the sen-
sations that were becoming part of her. She felt the
warmth and softness of the water wrapping her in liquid
silk; she smelled the provocative scent of the oil; she was
soothed by the sound of the gentle swish of water when
she moved. Melissa could feel the tension leaving her
body as though it were draining out of each pore, until
she became a part of the feel, the scent and the sound of
the water.

Eventually, her thoughts returned to her new neighbor and her unusual reaction to him. The look he'd given
her before dropping his gaze had been one of definite
male interest, which had surprised her. She wasn't used
to receiving looks of that nature. She considered herself
to be a scientist, first and foremost. Any stray thought
about her own sexuality was quickly relegated to that part
of her brain labeled Nonessential Information.

She frowned slightly. Why was that? she wondered.
Her thoughts lazily sought the elusive answer, trained to
accept any hypothesis and immediately go into action
seeking a satisfactory explanation.

Was it because she was an only child? Surely not.
Many people were only children, and they lived normal
lives. Ah, that was it. A normal life. When had her life
ever been considered normal?

Her parents had been pleasantly immersed in the world
of academia when she had unexpectedly made her entrance into the world. No doubt she had been a shock to
two dedicated people whose lives were devoted to theory
and research.

When had they discovered her unusual intelligence?
She had no way of knowing because she had never asked
the particulars surrounding her upbringing when they

were alive. Now, all she knew was what she could remember.

Her earliest memories were of classrooms where she was the youngest person. Her parents had made certain that she received the education she needed to spark her inquisitive mind. She recalled their pride in her, their encouragement to pursue her studies.

No one had suggested that she needed to learn how to interact with people her own age. She had finished her postgraduate work while still a teenager, too young and too inexperienced to know how to respond to the males with whom she came into contact.

Young, attractive men were alien to her way of life. She could not relate to them.

The problem was, Melissa admitted to herself, she didn't know how to respond to a man when he got that certain gleam of appreciation in his eye when he looked at her. Anyway, it didn't matter. Her new neighbor deserved to be treated with friendly courtesy. She doubted that they would see much of each other. Now that she'd thought about it, he hadn't even told her his name.

*I wonder what he does for a living?* She wriggled her toes in the water. *I wonder if he's married?* She grinned, amused by her wandering thoughts. What difference did it make? She was beginning to sound like her college roommate, whose entire life had been focused on the male species. Karen would no doubt have already figured a way to see the man again in order to get all her questions answered. There were times when Melissa wished she could be more like Karen—bubbly and outgoing, friendly as a puppy, totally unself-conscious.

When Melissa saw an attractive male, she immediately felt as though she were all elbows and knees, stammering, trying to think of something to say.

She had to face it. Her new neighbor was definitely attractive. Could it be possible that he was as shy as she? Only time would tell, and she had plenty of time.

Feeling better after her prolonged soak in the tub, Melissa reluctantly allowed the cooling water to drain from the tub. She grabbed a thick yellow towel that picked up the color scheme of her bathroom and briskly dried herself. Then she reached for her floor-length velour bathrobe, slipped it on and zipped it to the mandarin collar at her throat.

After vigorously brushing her hair out, Melissa started to the kitchen. Since she enjoyed working in the kitchen, she had long been in the habit of preparing and freezing meals on the weekends to eat when she got home after work during the week. She was trying to decide what she wanted for dinner when the doorbell rang.

She paused in the kitchen doorway, puzzled. Who could that possibly be? The insistent ringing reminded her that the best way to appease her curiosity would be to answer the door. Fighting a certain characteristic reluctance, Melissa walked over to the door and opened it.

Her neighbor stood in the hallway with a slight smile on his face, his hands in his pockets. "Hi! I'm sorry to bother you so soon, but you did offer to help me if I needed it." He paused, looking at her with appealing diffidence. His eyes stayed focused on hers. "The thing is . . ." He seemed to be searching for words.

Melissa realized that she was standing there barefoot, still in her robe, no doubt looking flushed from her recent bath. She could feel her color mounting once again.

"The thing is," he repeated hesitantly, "I was wondering if you would be able to tell me where the closest grocery store is located? I hate to get out and start driving without any idea where I'm headed."

"There's a store about three blocks from here," she offered with a slight smile.

"In which direction?"

She pointed without saying anything.

"Okay. Thanks."

She watched uncertainly as he turned away and started down the hallway. He'd almost reached the elevator before she was able to say, "Uh—excuse me?"

He glanced around.

"I, uh, was just about to warm up a casserole that's more than enough for two people. You're welcome to share it with me, if you'd like."

He stared at her as though he couldn't quite believe what he'd heard. "Are you inviting me to join you for dinner?"

Her cheeks felt as though they were on fire. "Only if you want to, of course."

Joel walked slowly toward her. "But you don't know me."

Now she was feeling like a complete fool. "Well, yes, I'm aware of that. However, I know that if you passed the rigid screening done by the management of the building, you're all right."

He stopped in front of her. "You're very trusting, aren't you?"

Suddenly Melissa realized how foolish she was being. "You're right. It was a stupid thing to do."

"No, wait," he said, placing his hand on the door. "Don't get me wrong. I'd really enjoy sharing a home-cooked meal, believe me. You just caught me off guard, that's all."

Melissa didn't know how to respond. He saved her from the necessity of a reply by stepping past her into her apartment.

The impulse to invite him in had shocked her. His acceptance of the invitation completely unnerved her. Slowly, Melissa closed the door, then turned to face him.

"I didn't get a chance to introduce myself, earlier. I'm Joel Kramer. And I think it's very kind of you to invite me to dinner. Thank you." He pushed his glasses up slightly where they rested on the bridge of his nose.

Once again, she noticed an endearing shyness in this man that gave her some much-needed confidence. "I'm glad you decided to accept my offer. I get tired of eating alone," she admitted with a smile.

Trying to hide her nervousness, she motioned him toward the arrangement of sofa and chairs in the living area of her apartment.

He glanced around the room, then looked back at her. "I like the way you have your place arranged. I hope I can manage to get my place into something as livable. The movers set everything in each room without any attempt to arrange the stuff comfortably." He stopped talking, but continued to look at her with a quizzical expression on his face. Melissa realized she was still standing by the front door.

"Have a seat," she managed to say in a jerky voice, "and I'll put the casserole on." She felt a certain sense of relief as soon as she disappeared into the kitchen. What had she been thinking of, asking him to stay for dinner? Didn't she have any sense at all? She didn't know the man, and she didn't have a clue how to make casual conversation.

Melissa peeked around the doorway. He was studying one of the paintings on her wall.

Melissa took a deep breath. There was no harm in being neighborly, after all, she pointed out to herself. She would feed him and then he would go home. There was no reason to think that he would see her offer as anything but a neighborly gesture.

She hoped.

"Would you like a glass of wine?" she asked.

He turned abruptly to face her, and she realized that he wasn't as relaxed as he'd first appeared. "If you're having one."

She nodded. "I have a nice Rhine, or cabernet sauvignon. Do you have a preference?"

"Not really. Whatever you're having."

Melissa forced herself to take a deep breath, then slowly exhaled. She placed the casserole in the oven, poured two glasses of wine and returned to the living room.

"Aren't your feet cold?" he asked, taking one of the glasses.

She nodded. "I just got out of the tub when you rang. If you'll excuse me for a moment, I'll get dressed."

"Sure." He sat down and watched her go through a door that he assumed led to her bedroom.

Joel sipped the wine, enjoying the fruity flavor and the slight tingle on his tongue. After glancing at the closed bedroom door, he rose quietly and soundlessly moved to the window. With practiced ease, he edged the blind aside enough to look down at the street.

The nondescript car that had followed Melissa home was still there, parked across from the building. He'd spotted the tail shortly after she arrived. He'd reported the license-plate number to Max before he hurried into the hall to greet his new neighbor. Hopefully, he'd have a little more to go on before long.

Was Dr. Jordan aware that she'd been followed? He couldn't tell. Joel moved back to his chair and sat down, deliberately assuming a posture of nonchalance, and waited for her to appear once more. An assignment watching an attractive woman who invited him to join her for a home-cooked meal definitely had its positive side. This assignment certainly beat the last one down in Central America.

The bedroom door opened, and Melissa appeared wearing a royal-blue running suit the color of her eyes.

Joel smiled at her. Now that he was adjusting to being around her, he realized that he'd have to remember to thank Max for the assignment. He didn't think he was going to mind looking after Melissa Jordan at all.

She sat down across from him and nervously sipped her wine. She'd been rehearsing possible conversational gambits while she dressed, but now her mind was a total blank.

"Have you lived here long?" Joel asked after the silence had stretched out for several minutes.

"A little over five years." Melissa took another sip of her wine, hoping it would relax her.

"Are you from Virginia?"

"No. Massachusetts."

Another long silence stretched between them.

"Where do you—"

"Do you work—" They both spoke at once, then stopped.

"What were you—"

"Go ahead and—" Again, they spoke together.

Joel began to laugh, an infectious chuckle that caused a ripple of awareness to flow through Melissa. Once again, she could feel her color changing. She detested her thin skin that so quickly betrayed her emotions.

"What were you going to say?" Joel asked with a grin.

Melissa brushed an errant curl away from her cheek. "Oh. I was just going to ask you where you were from."

Joel always had a cover story for every assignment, but since this particular job was unlike his usual situations, he made the decision to stick to the truth as much as possible.

"I lived on a ranch in Colorado until I went away to college."

"Oh. Your father is a rancher?"

"No. I was raised by my grandparents. My mother died before I was school age. My dad traveled a lot, so he left me with my mother's family."

Although his explanation sounded matter-of-fact, Melissa wondered if he'd been as lonely growing up as she had been. "Were you an only child?"

"Yes." He tasted the wine before asking, "How about you?"

"Yes. My parents were in their late thirties when I was born."

He smiled. "That gives us something in common, at least. Being an only child can be lonely at times, can't it?"

So he *did* understand. Somehow, that made her feel closer to him. "I managed to stay occupied," she admitted.

"Me, too. Since the family owned a working ranch, I spent most of my time out of doors."

Melissa recognized the divergence of their childhoods with his statement. She had spent most of her youth with her nose buried in books.

"What do you do?" she finally asked, wondering if there was any such thing as ranching this far east.

"I'm a writer," he explained in a casual voice. "And you?"

She shrugged. "I work for a pharmaceutical company."

He noticed that she didn't elaborate on what she did there, and he wondered if he should push. Why not? "Doing what?" Ah, that had caught her unaware. He watched as she hesitated, obviously searching for a casual response.

"I, uh, work in the research-and-development lab."

"Oh, all the hush-hush experiments, huh?"

"Nothing so exciting, I'm afraid. Mostly I deal with the mounds of paperwork regarding what doesn't work." Her smile made light of her words.

At least her answer confirmed what Feldman had told them. He began to understand Feldman's concern. There was no denying that she had been followed home. If someone attempted to interrogate her, she would not be in any position to respond.

"What do you write about?" she asked, bringing him back to the present.

This part he had already decided upon, picking a genre that he enjoyed reading whenever he found the time. "I'm working on a Western."

She cocked her head. "And you moved to Virginia?"

Watch it, Kramer. This woman's sharp. "Actually, I've lived on the eastern seaboard since I graduated from college. Any research information I need can be easily picked up at a local library."

"Do you ever visit Colorado?"

"No. The ranch was sold years ago. There's no one there to visit. How about you? Do you ever go to Massachusetts?"

She shook her head. "My family's gone, too."

He leaned forward in his chair. "So we're both alone in the world."

"You make us sound like forsaken orphans."

He grinned. "What I was thinking was that maybe we should adopt each other. Maybe we won't find the world so lonely."

She looked at him uncertainly, wondering if he was teasing her, wishing she understood people better. "I'm not sure I need adopting at this age," she admitted.

"Yeah, I know what you mean. So what if we just become friends?"

"I don't have much time for friendships."

"Neither do I," Joel admitted, wondering if he'd ever really thought about that aspect of his life before. He'd never needed or wanted friends once he finished college. In his business, friendship could get you killed.

"You write at home?"

"Yes."

"No wonder you're lonely. What do you do for fun?"

He thought about all the possible quips he could throw her way, but decided against them. She looked so serious, as though she truly wanted to know. He dredged up memories of what he enjoyed doing when he had a few days to himself. "I love to walk along the beach. I do a little sailing when I can. I feel a real affinity to water."

Her expression grew wistful. "That sounds fun."

"Maybe you'd like to go with me sometime," he responded, his mind busy with the opportunity to get her away from this area for a while, at least until Max checked out possible causes of Dr. Feldman's accident.

"I don't know. At the moment, my boss is on vacation, so things are a little hectic for me."

He finished his wine. "Well, you can think about it and let me know if you can get away. We could always plan something for next weekend."

"Isn't it too cold for sailing?"

"I was thinking more about going to the seashore. Have you ever watched a storm come in over the ocean? It's really awesome."

A sudden buzzing sound startled him and he glanced around.

"Oh, that's the timer. Our dinner's ready." She leaped up as though relieved to be able to change the subject.

Joel followed her more slowly into the kitchen. She was wary, there was no getting around that. But then, he hadn't expected this job to be easy. He sighed. At least he'd made contact. The next thing was to insinuate himself into her daily life. He didn't consider that task would work much of a hardship on him.

"What can I do to help?" he asked as he joined her, savoring the delicious aroma rising from the steaming casserole she'd set on the cabinet.

Joel had to remind himself that he was being paid for carrying out this assignment!

## Chapter Two

The first thing Joel did when he returned to his apartment after dinner was to look out the window. The car he had seen earlier was gone. In its place was another nondescript car of an equally neutral color. He reached for his binoculars and waited until the lights of a passing car illuminated the license-plate number of the latest arrival, then he jotted down the number.

The second thing he did, still without putting on a light, was pick up the phone and punch out Max's number on the glowing handset.

"Yes?"

"I have another license number for you to check," he said without identifying himself.

"Let's hear it."

He repeated the numbers. "Have you got anything on the first one?"

"Other than the fact the car's registered to a dummy corporation? No, but we're hoping the lead is going to take us somewhere. We're currently checking out the corporate name for possible use in other areas, as well.''

"I don't like it, Max. Nobody is going to spend their days and nights sitting out in this cold just to admire a good-looking blonde.''

"Oh she is, is she?''

Joel realized what he'd said and, for a moment, found himself without a reply. Finally he spoke. "As a matter of fact, she's very attractive.''

"Hmm. Still want off the case?''

"Very funny.''

"Have you made contact with her yet?''

Joel grinned. Without hiding his satisfaction, he replied, "As a matter of fact, she and I had dinner together... at her place.''

"Fast work.''

"I'll admit I lucked out. I understand why Feldman was concerned about her, though. I don't think she has a clue that something could be wrong or that she was followed. As much as I appreciated the dinner invitation, I think she's much too trusting of people she doesn't know.''

Max chuckled. "Why do I get a picture of sending the wolf to look after Little Red Riding Hood?''

"Poor joke, Max. This thing could turn bad real fast.''

"We had the earlier car ticketed. We'll get rid of this one the same way.''

"They'll just try another method. I'm going to provide taxi service for her from now until this matter is cleared up.''

"I'm impressed. How did you manage to convince her that she needed an escort service?''

"Well, actually, I'm just going to be a friendly neighbor offering her a ride in the morning when her car won't start. We'll play it from there...maybe have the car towed to a garage, play around with things like parts on order, shorthanded in the shop, missing invoice ticket, that sort of thing.''

"If you think it will work.''

"It's the best I can think of on short notice. What I really want to do is to get her out of town. Any chance of that?''

"We're talking to the company officials about closing down for a few weeks until we can sort this affair out.''

"Isn't that playing into the hands of whoever is behind this?''

"Maybe. But if they aren't aware we're on to them, we've got a chance to stop them before somebody gets killed. These people mean business. You, of all people, should remember that.''

Joel shivered, remembering the condition he'd been in when he'd returned to the States from his last assignment. "Yeah, I know.''

"Just stick close to your charge. We'll take care of the rest.''

Joel dropped the receiver back into its cradle and headed toward the bedroom. He was pleased with the results of his first encounter with Melissa Jordan. She had bought his story of being a writer. So far, so good. All he needed to do was to make himself available whenever she needed assistance. He'd make sure he was in the parking garage when she left for work tomorrow. After that, he'd count on his luck to get him through the following hours.

*Wouldn't you know the morning I oversleep, everything would go wrong,* Melissa thought, jerking off the second pair of pantyhose she'd tried on that morning, only to discover a run in them, too.

Impatiently, she grabbed an unopened package and successfully completed dressing. She ignored the growling of her stomach. By skipping breakfast, she would at least be able to put herself back on schedule, traffic permitting.

With her coat and purse in one hand, she hastily locked the front door and sprinted for the elevator. For once, it responded promptly and she began to relax on the way to the basement. Everything was all right now, she decided, pulling on her coat and lifting the hood around her ears.

She waved at one of her neighbors as she stepped out of the elevator and hurried to her car. As soon as she slid into the front seat, she jammed the key into the ignition and turned it.

Nothing happened.

Oh, no! She turned it a couple more times. Nothing. No! She couldn't have car trouble now, of all times. She had to get to work. With Dr. Feldman being gone, she—

"Hi. Having trouble?"

She glanced around and saw Joel standing by the car, looking in. "It looks like it."

"You want me to check on it?"

"Oh, would you, please?" She released the hood, and he obligingly studied the engine, the distributor cap he'd disconnected the night before, the loosened battery cables. Then he walked back around to her.

"I don't know all that much about cars, but it looks like you may have a faulty distributor cap."

She groaned, closing her eyes.

"Could I give you a ride somewhere?"

"Oh, if you wouldn't mind, I'd certainly appreciate it. I really need to get to work."

He opened the car door and held out his hand to her. "No problem. I was on my way to the grocery store to lay in some supplies. Good thing I happened to see you." He led her over to his car, helped her into the passenger seat, then got in on the driver's side.

"You'll have to give me directions," he said, which she quickly did. "If you'd like, I'll see that your car gets to a garage."

"Oh, I hate to put you to so much trouble."

"Hey, that's what friends and neighbors are for."

Melissa couldn't resist his open, friendly smile. What a nice man: uncomplicated, wholesome, straightforward, easy to know. After spending the previous evening with him, she felt as though she'd known him for years. He considered his life boring, but she was impressed with how comfortable he was with himself. He knew what he wanted, and what he wanted was to write. Nothing wrong with that. Melissa found him to be a refreshing change from the ambitious people who made up her contacts in life. Compared to Joel, everyone she knew, herself included, was driven—working long hours, neglecting their health. Just look at Dr. Feldman. She knew he wouldn't be able to enjoy his vacation. He'd probably spend the entire time recuperating from the flu.

No doubt she could learn a great deal from being around Joel Kramer. When he glanced around at her again, she returned his smile.

"Warm enough?"

"I'm fine. Thank you for the ride. You're a real lifesaver."

"If you'll let me know when you get off work, I'll be here to pick you up."

"That's all right. I can call a cab."

"Why? There's no need to spend the money when I'm available."

"But won't it cut into your writing time?"

He shook his head. "I've probably done all I'm going to do today. I'm a morning person. I've been up for hours, working."

"Oh. Well, if you're sure you don't mind."

"I would consider it a privilege. Then maybe you'll have dinner with me. That's the least I can do for last night."

She eyed him uncertainly. "Dinner?"

"Nothing fancy," he assured her. "I found a restaurant not far from the apartments that serves tasty meals. It will save us both from having to cook tonight."

They pulled up in front of the building she pointed out. When she opened her door, he placed his hand gently on her arm. "Please? Take pity on a newcomer to town, all right?"

His silver-eyed gaze seemed to melt her heart. Whether he wanted to admit it or not, she thought, Joel was lonely. She smiled. "All right. I should be through around six." Melissa slipped out of the car before she could change her mind.

He waved. "See you then," he replied with a nod, and pulled away from the curb.

The cold wind whipped around her legs and she shivered. She hurried into the sprawling building, her mind already on the tasks that awaited her.

Joel pulled up to the first pay phone he could find and called Max to make arrangements to pick up Melissa's car. Max would see that it got a good tune-up and was effectively unavailable until Joel knew what he was going to do with Melissa Jordan.

If some of the dreams he'd had the night before were any indication, his active imagination had come up with several possibilities.

Melissa spotted Joel's car as soon as she stepped outside the building that evening. He saw her at the same time and climbed out, so that by the time she reached his side, the passenger door stood open, waiting for her. The cold wind kept them from lingering, and she didn't greet him with more than a smile until he sat down beside her in the car.

"What a treat, having a warm car waiting for me at the end of the day."

He grinned. "Hope you're hungry. I got busy and forgot to eat lunch, so I'm starved."

"How's the book going?" she asked.

"Who knows? I just keep putting words on paper and refuse to evaluate them until I get the story down."

She smiled. "That sounds sensible to me. Where are we going to eat?"

He named a restaurant she'd heard of but had never visited. Melissa couldn't believe how happy she felt at the moment, having an attractive male pick her up from work and take her out to dinner. She didn't really understand what was happening to her. Where had her reservations about social activities gone? She didn't know. All she was certain of was the fact that her day had been just as hectic as yesterday, but because she knew that she had plans for the evening, she had breezed through the details, done her work with a crisp clarity and walked out of the lab with a buoyant step and a light heart.

She felt proud of herself. In the past, she'd thought of herself as socially inept, but last night she had proven herself wrong. She had met someone, been friendly with him, and a friendship was forming as a result of her daring to act in a way that was different from her normal response.

"How was your day?" Joel asked.

Melissa glanced around at him. His tone and expression gave every indication that he really wanted to know, despite the banality of the question.

Unfortunately, she couldn't discuss her work with anyone outside of the lab, but it was thoughtful of him to ask. "Like most jobs, everywhere, I guess," she responded with a smile.

"Do you like what you do?"

"Very much."

He reached over and touched her hand that rested in her lap. "I'm glad. I think it's important that a person earn their living in the way they enjoy."

They rode the rest of the way to the restaurant in a companionable silence.

From the time they entered the restaurant until they left, their conversation flowed easily and Melissa's sense of comfort and relaxation continued to grow. She couldn't recall all that was said because they discussed so many things—books, movies, American policies and political attitudes, their favorite foods, hobbies.

What they discovered was that they were alike in many ways, and both were absorbed in their work with little time for outside activities.

By the time they reached their respective apartments, they were chatting as though they'd known each other for years.

"What do you have planned for this evening?" he asked, taking her key from her and opening her door.

"The usual, I guess. Read awhile and go to bed."

"I rented some movies while I was at the store this morning. Want to come over and watch one with me?"

Melissa could feel her heart pick up its tempo. It would be so easy to grow accustomed to having this man around. "Haven't you had enough of me, yet?"

The look he gave her caused the hated heat to fill her cheeks. "I don't believe that could ever happen, Melissa," he said in a barely audible voice.

She studied him in silence for a moment. She'd just been congratulating herself earlier on making new, bold decisions. Now was the time for another one. Could she do it?

"All right. Let me change into something more comfortable and I'll be over in a few minutes."

"Okay. I'll see you later, then."

He waited for her to close her door before going inside his own apartment. Good. Having her over here would keep her close for another evening. He glanced around the room, making sure everything had been put away. He stopped off in the small second bedroom to make certain it looked as though a writer had been busy. A small computer sat on the desk, a couple of reference books nearby. The printer had paper fed into the tractor, ready to go.

When he reached his bedroom, he picked up a towel he'd tossed down earlier and threw it into the bathroom. Not that he expected for her to see his bedroom. As much as he would enjoy taking her to bed, he knew better. She was his current assignment, that was all. He could find his pleasure elsewhere.

The sound of a soft tap on the front door drew him back into the living room. He opened the door with a smile, saw the expression on her face and immediately asked, "What's wrong?"

Melissa came into the room. "I wish I knew. I just got a call from the personnel director of the plant. It seems our office building failed some sort of inspection. The explanation doesn't make much sense to me. But, for whatever reason I'm supposed to take the rest of the week off."

Joel grinned. "No kidding. That's great."

Melissa had wandered over to his bookshelves while she talked, and she looked around in surprise at his response. "What's so great about it?"

He shrugged, slipping his hands into his pockets. "Well, now you can have a minivacation."

She smiled at him, as though amused at his obvious misunderstanding of the situation. "I suppose so, but, you see, I don't want a minivacation. I enjoy my job very much. I don't need to do anything else."

He wandered over to her, his hands still in his pockets. "When was the last time you took some time off?"

She thought about that for a moment, then shrugged. "I don't remember. We take the normal holidays off, like most businesses."

"I mean a vacation."

She turned away from him and walked over to the window. Without looking at him, she said, "I don't really like vacations." She glanced around at him and smiled. "I find them boring, actually." She tilted her chin slightly, as though expecting him to argue the point.

He noticed her tension but couldn't understand its cause. In a careful tone Joel offered, "I suppose that depends on what you enjoy doing to relax."

Melissa turned away from the window in a restless movement. She found the present topic of conversation unsettling, almost irritating, although she didn't know why. "I don't need to relax," she explained. "I enjoy my job. I find it fulfills all my needs. I've never been one to find pleasure in lying around doing nothing.''

To stop her restless movements, Joel took her hand and led her over to the sofa in front of the television. Motioning for her to sit down, he sat beside her and turned so that he was facing her. ''Who said that a vacation has to be about doing nothing? The whole idea is to do something different. It's a chance to pursue other interests, other hobbies, that sort of thing.''

Her gaze returned to the window for a moment, then she shook her head. ''This really isn't the time of year for outdoor activities.''

''Sure it is, if you enjoy skiing.'' Personally, he hated the sport; no doubt because he was lousy at it.

''I don't enjoy cold weather.''

He grinned. ''Me, either.'' He leaned back and rested his head on the back of the sofa, thinking. ''My idea of a perfect winter vacation is to go somewhere warm, preferably a beach somewhere.'' He closed his eyes. ''Just think about it. A chance to soak up some sun, do a little swimming, maybe snorkeling, find a sailboat somewhere.'' He smiled to himself. ''Now that's my idea of living.'' He raised his head and looked at her. ''Haven't you ever wanted just to forget about everything in your life and run away for a few days?''

She looked at him warily. ''No.''

''Haven't you ever done anything on the spur of the moment?''

''Not really, no. I'm more comfortable thinking everything through.''

''You know, Melissa, I think that it's time that you create some excitement in your life.''

''Why?''

He stared at her. "Why? You have to ask me why? By the very fact that you can ask such a question shows me that you are in much worse shape than I first thought." He reached over and took her hand, as though comforting her. "You, my dear neighbor, obviously have been deprived of some of the most delicious moments of life—those little unexpected, unplanned moments, the serendipities that add magic to a person's life." He brought her hand up and placed it against his cheek. With a flash of his smile, he said, "Why don't you run away with me for a few days, Melissa? Live a little...take a chance on life."

She stared at him with obvious bewilderment. "Are you serious?"

"Never more serious in my life."

"You want to just run off somewhere...?" She eyed him uncertainly. "Where?"

He shrugged. "You name it, we'll go."

She stared at him for several moments in silence and discovered within her a yearning to be the kind of person that could do something so impulsive. But, of course, she couldn't. She didn't even know the man. It was one thing to have dinner with him a couple of times. It was another thing entirely to run away with him.

With surprising reluctance, she shook her head. "I'm sorry. But I can't." She softened her refusal with a smile.

Joel stood and walked over to the VCR. Keeping his back to her, he answered in a casual tone of voice. "What are you in the mood to watch tonight? I can offer you a comedy, drama or an action adventure."

"I thought you had to write your book."

He glanced around at her with a puzzled expression on his face. "Watching a movie isn't going to prevent me from finishing my book."

She grinned. "I meant if you were to go away for a few days."

"Oh!" He shrugged. "I can work anywhere. But you're right. You don't know me. It was a crazy idea."

She shook her head. "I didn't mean to be rude. I'm afraid that I don't know the proper social etiquette surrounding an invitation to share a vacation."

"Neither do I," he admitted. "I've never done it before."

Melissa's eyes widened slightly. "That surprises me."

"Why should it? Do I strike you as the kind of guy who invites every attractive woman he meets to take a trip with him?"

Melissa could hear the irritation in his voice and realized that she was in way over her head. She hadn't meant to be insulting. She just didn't know what to say, how to behave or what to do next. She also found the news that he thought she was attractive more than a little unnerving.

"I didn't mean to offend you," she said after a moment. She watched as he took a long breath and sharply exhaled.

"Forget it. I didn't mean to be so touchy. The thing is, I'm really not trying to come on to you. I just thought it would give us a chance to get to know each other a little better, that's all. Talking about the idea made me realize that I haven't taken any time off this winter, either. I guess one of the reasons I haven't planned anything is because it's not much fun to go somewhere alone." Joel ran his hand through his hair, wanting to change the subject. He looked at the tape in his hand. "So, what sounds good to you?" He read off the names of three movies.

Melissa picked one and he placed the tape in the machine, set it in motion and sat down beside her once again.

Before long, Melissa appeared to be engrossed in the movie. Although he'd never seen it before, Joel found his thoughts drifting, going back to their conversation. For a short while, he'd forgotten the role he'd been playing and had taken her rejection of his offer personally, which was total nonsense. So what had caused him to react like that?

Perhaps it was because he could see the parallels in their lives. He couldn't remember the last time he'd taken a vacation and for the same reasons she had given him. His work was his life, his hobby, his recreation. However, when he heard her expressing a similar point of view, he immediately saw how one-dimensional such an attitude could be. Like him, she refused to consider other attitudes. He'd never looked at his own attitudes from another's perspective before. He wasn't sure he liked them.

He thought of a recent conversation he'd had with Max. His employer had suggested he take a few weeks off. Joel had been furious at the suggestion, demanding that he be given another assignment as soon as possible.

Melissa chuckled, bringing Joel back to the movie. He'd missed whatever she'd found amusing. He needed to pay attention. They might discuss the movie later and he didn't want her to think he'd been bored.

How could he be bored when he was so aware of the woman sitting within arm's reach of him? She'd changed into a pair of faded jeans and a bulky knit sweater. She'd brushed her hair out when she'd changed clothes and had left it hanging loose. One long curl fell across her shoulder and Joel had to resist the impulse to twine the soft mass around his finger. He finally admitted to himself that he'd wanted to run his hands through her hair since the first time he'd seen it down the night before.

*This is a job, Kramer. Remember that.*

He managed to see the humor in what was happening on the screen when Melissa began to laugh a few minutes later, and he joined in. The sound of their shared laughter sounded companionable, and Joel began to relax a little. Did it really matter if she chose to stay home? He could watch her as effectively here as anywhere. She'd be a lot safer in the apartment building than traveling to and from work. Somehow he'd have to find ways where they could spend large chunks of time together.

After all, what was wrong with making friends with her? He wasn't there spying on her. He was there to look after her. He could become friends with her without compromising his work.

"Could I get you something to drink?" he asked, suddenly remembering his role as host.

She smiled, her eyes filled with amusement at the story unfolding on the screen. "Thank you. I'd like that."

"I have beer, wine and soft drinks."

She named a popular cola drink and he left the room. "Don't you want to stop the movie?" she called after him.

"No need. I'll be right back."

Within a couple of minutes, he returned with two ice-filled glasses, the sparkling cola making soft hissing noises.

He watched her take a drink from the glass, watched the way the moisture beaded on her upper lip, watched as she licked the moisture away with the tip of her tongue. All the while, her attention stayed with the movie.

Joel forced his gaze back to the screen. Damn, but he found her attractive. Sitting this close, he'd noticed a spray of freckles across the bridge of her nose…and the way her bottom lip protruded ever so slightly in an innocently provocative pout. He'd never seen eyelashes as long as hers. He was fascinated by the way they brushed against her cheek when she looked down at her drink.

When she turned her head to look at him, he refused to avert his gaze.

"Is something wrong?" she asked.

He shook his head. "On the contrary. I find you fascinating." He smiled as a fiery blush filled her cheeks. "I'm sorry. I didn't mean to embarrass you. Surely you must know how attractive you are. The men in your life aren't blind."

When she just stared at him, he reached over and very gently rubbed his thumb against her cheek. "Hmm. Your skin feels like a baby's." He rested his head against the back of the sofa and watched as the pupils in her eyes seemed to grow. She sat very still.

He leaned slowly toward her, not wanting to frighten her, but wanting very much to touch her again. After slipping his hand from her cheek to the nape of her neck, he massaged the tenseness he felt there, then with a calm deliberation, he placed his lips against hers.

Just before his mouth touched hers, he felt more than heard her soft gasp. But she didn't pull away. Her parted lips invited him to explore, but he could already feel her trembling. Was it possible that she was afraid of him? Or was she afraid of the intimacy of the moment?

He lifted his head slightly and looked into her eyes. "I won't take advantage of you. Please believe that," he whispered. "You can stop me at any time."

He watched as her impossibly long lashes drooped across her expressive eyes. Then he closed his eyes, as well. He took his time, touching his lips to hers once again, then against her closed eyelids, against her cheek, her brow, then returning to taste her once more.

She sighed, and with a hesitancy he found endearing, she slipped her arms around his neck, pulling him closer.

He wrapped his other arm around her, holding her tightly against him. He continued to kiss her—soft, nipping kisses, tantalizing and teasing her with his light touch until she shifted restlessly in his arms.

He knew he needed to let her go, but found the task impossible. Instead, the energy changed between them. There was a new urgency. Their kiss deepened, became more possessive, and Joel lost all sense of what he'd originally intended when he first touched her.

Restlessly he spread his hands along her spine, wanting to draw her even closer to him. She leaned her head back, giving him access to the long slim line of her throat. Dear God, but she was beautiful, and he wanted her with an urgency that shook him.

"Melissa," he whispered, shaken. "I . . ."

She slowly opened her eyes, looking as dazed as he felt. "Joel?"

"Hmmmm?"

"I don't think this is a very good idea."

Funny how her admitting what he'd just been thinking was not as comforting as he could have wished. He reluctantly released her. "I'm sorry. I shouldn't have—"

"Oh, please don't apologize. You didn't do anything wrong. It's just that . . ." She paused and rubbed her forehead. "I'm not very good at this sort of thing. And I wouldn't want us to hurt a friendship by moving it along too fast." Her look was beseeching.

Joel stood and moved away from the couch. He needed to get a safe distance between them. "I agree."

The movie ended and the credits rolled. "Well..." Melissa came to her feet. "I guess I'd better go. It's getting late." She looked at Joel, who was standing beside the window looking outside. He turned toward her at the sound of her voice.

"Thanks for coming over." He didn't move closer to her.

"I forgot to ask about my car. Did they say when it would be ready?"

"No. They said they'd call. I gave them my number since I didn't know yours."

"Oh."

They continued to look at each other.

Finally Melissa spoke. "Since I don't have to work tomorrow, maybe we could do something together. That is, if you still want to plan something."

Joel smiled at her. "I'd like that. I'd like that very much."

She returned his smile. "Me, too."

He walked over to where she stood beside the door. "What would you like to do?" Without conscious thought, he rubbed his knuckle lightly against her cheek.

"I don't care."

"I'll think of something."

They stood there, just inches apart, as though neither one wanted to be the first to end their time together. Joel leaned down and kissed her lightly on her lips, then said, "I'll walk you home."

She chuckled. "I'm just across the hall."

"I know." He opened the door and followed her through, then waited while she unlocked her door. "This way, I can tell you good-night," he whispered, taking her into his arms once more and kissing her with all the pent-up emotion that had been gathering within him.

Melissa responded by sliding her arms around his neck. Having a neighbor like Joel Kramer had certainly turned her life upside down, but she was determined not to allow her shyness to keep her from experiencing all he had to offer.

# Chapter Three

"When was the last time you explored D.C.?" Joel asked. He and Melissa were approaching the entrance to the Washington Monument.

She shook her head. "I can't remember. I think there was a group of us from school that came down one summer."

Joel pulled her closer by tucking her hand inside his pocket. "Everything looks different in the wintertime, anyway."

"I've always wanted to come when the cherry trees were in bloom, but somehow the time slipped away from me."

"The Potomac Park would be another place to go in the spring for that reason."

Melissa looked around her and sighed. "This was a great idea you had. I'm glad you insisted."

"Otherwise you would be curled up in your apartment reading a book."

"Maybe. Or I might have taken a walk."

"So you're getting your exercise and exploring the country's capital at the same time. You can't beat that."

Within a couple of hours, Joel suggested lunch. Melissa readily agreed. The exercise had stirred her appetite.

They found a cozy tearoom that intrigued Melissa with its delicate decorations. Joel had gamely agreed to try the cuisine.

"What do you think of the soup?" Melissa asked after they were served.

"I like it," Joel replied. "How about the salad?"

"Marvelous. Here," she offered him a bite. "Try it."

Joel obligingly opened his mouth, chewed and swallowed with a smile. "Great house dressing. Here, try the soup."

Melissa leaned on her palm and looked at the man across from her. "You know, I've never known anyone like you."

Joel glanced up from his steaming bowl. "Is that good or bad?"

She smiled. "Good. You're really so much fun to be with. You didn't quibble when I dragged you into this feminine atmosphere for lunch."

He glanced around the room. "I'm not the only male here. Obviously, the food doesn't recognize genders."

"I have a hunch you wouldn't have cared if you'd been the only man here. That's what I'm talking about. You're comfortable wherever you go."

"Aren't you?"

She shook her head. "I've always been dreadfully self-conscious."

"About what?"

She shrugged. "Of being me, I guess. I always felt like a freak."

Joel placed his spoon beside his plate and looked at her with raised eyebrows. "Would you care to explain that remark?"

"As far back as I can remember, I went to classes with students several years older than I was. My parents encouraged me to study and learn, and I wanted to please them. Consequently, I never felt accepted by any of my peers in school. Outside of discussions about homework, we never had anything in common." She took another bite of salad.

"Didn't you make friends with people your own age?"

"No. We lived in an older residential area, so that I was the youngest child on the block. Children my age that I did meet seemed to be uncomfortable around me."

"So you never learned how to play."

"Not really."

"Talk about a lonely childhood. At least I had friends from neighboring ranches to play with. My grandparents were lenient with me, provided I did my share of the chores. I had a great group of friends."

"Do you see any of them now?"

Joel was quiet for several moments. "No. Two of them were killed in Vietnam. I lost touch with the other ones once the ranch sold."

"The only person that I consider a friend from my younger days was my college roommate. She lives in New York but stays in touch. Karen's always trying to get me to join her and her family when they go on vacation."

"She's married?"

"Yes. She's several years older than I am. She married the summer after graduation. I went on for more degrees while she got started with a family." Melissa smiled. "I'm much better at acquiring degrees than I am experiencing life."

Joel leaned back in his chair and observed her with a whimsical smile. "Oh, I don't know about that. You haven't done so badly since I've known you."

"You've made it easy for me. You're very comfortable to be around, you know."

"You're the first person to have noticed that particular aspect of my personality."

Melissa studied his amused expression. With a serious expression of her own, she explained, "I've always considered myself hopeless in social situations. I never know what to say or how to act."

He smiled at her. "Be yourself."

"Like you do..." She paused, thinking about it. "I'd like to be able to do that. Usually, I can never find anything to say. And yet with you, I don't seem to ever stop talking."

"I consider that to be a compliment."

They smiled at each other.

"So, what do you want to do this afternoon?" Joel asked a short while later over coffee.

"Continue playing tourist. I want to see the White House, the Capitol, the Jefferson Memorial, the Lincoln Memorial, the Smithsonian—"

Joel began to laugh. "Whoa, whoa, wait a minute. We might be able to drive by some of those places, but the Smithsonian would take days to explore."

Her smile was filled with anticipation. "I've got at least the rest of the week off." Then she remembered. "But you have to write, don't you?"

He nodded. "But if we plan it, I can do both. I try to get three hours a day of writing done. Since I don't need much sleep, I get up early. We could leave around ten or so each day and still see a considerable amount.''

"And you'd be willing to do that with me?''

"Of course. We're friends, remember?''

Melissa looked at him, knowing full well that she would always remember. Meeting Joel was an experience she would never forget. She would store each event she shared with him like a souvenir to recall later.

Impulsively, she reached over and placed her hand on top of his. "Thank you.''

"For what?''

"For being you.''

"I'm glad you picked a warmer day to visit Chesapeake Bay,'' Melissa said ten days later. She glanced up at the blue sky, then back at the large expanse of water before them.

Joel stood with his hands in his pockets, gazing out into the bay. "I have to confess I've been watching the weather map for the last few days, trying to plan a trip over here that wouldn't be uncomfortable.''

She threw her arms out and spun around. "You think of everything, don't you?''

"I try,'' he responded modestly, then ruined it by rakishly grinning at her. When she stopped turning and looked at him, he grabbed her around the waist and swung her around in a circle, causing her to laugh. When he stopped, he held her close to him.

"You sound like a little girl when you laugh like that.''

"I feel like a little girl when you continue to indulge me the way you have these last couple of weeks. At this rate, you're never going to get your book finished.''

"Don't worry about my book. I'm certainly not.''

"Aren't you writing on some sort of schedule?''

"Not really. I decided to give myself a full year to see what I could do with my writing. I have several months to go."

"What did you do before you began writing?"

"A very boring desk job. One you wouldn't want to spend time hearing about."

"I can't think of anything about you that I would find boring."

"Why, Dr. Jordan, I'm flattered."

She laughed again, the young, free sound of happiness echoing around them. "You have no idea how much I've enjoyed myself. It's as though you had to teach me how to play. I'd never before realized how serious I am about everything." She waved her hand at the scene around them. "I would never have thought to come here at this time of year."

"We managed to beat a great deal of the traffic by getting here a few months early."

"I really need to write Karen and let her know that I finally took her advice. Who knows? I might go with them down to the islands this summer when they go."

"The islands?"

"Yes. She and her husband have a place on one of the smaller islands in the Virgin Islands chain."

He dropped his arm across her shoulder and they headed back toward the car. "Too bad they don't go now, when the weather's so cold here at home."

"I know. But Tony can't ever seem to get away during the winter and Karen won't go without him."

Joel helped Melissa into his car. "Where do you want to go now?"

She glanced at her watch. "Oh, darn. It's too late to pick up my car. They promised it would be ready this afternoon."

"There's no hurry, is there?"

"Hurry! You must be joking. They could have rebuilt the entire car in the time it's taken them to replace the distributor cap and tune it."

"You know how busy auto shops are."

"Well, at least I can get it tomorrow. I'm sure you'll be relieved not to have to drive me everywhere."

"Actually, I thought I'd done a very good job of playing chauffeur. If this book doesn't sell, I'm counting on your good references to find another job."

Melissa loved to watch the light dance in his eyes whenever he teased her. And he teased her a great deal, another thing she loved. She sat beside him and watched as he smoothly shifted gears, his hands resting lightly on the gear shift and the steering wheel.

She felt as though she had known this man forever. Over the past couple of weeks, they had shared so many of their childhood memories with each other. She felt as though she had been there with him as he grew up on the ranch in Colorado. Now when she recalled her solitary childhood, it felt as though he had also been there in the background, encouraging her.

"What are you thinking?" he asked.

She leaned her head against the headrest and smiled. "About you and how fortunate it was for me that you became my neighbor. I'm really glad I met you."

He reached over and touched her hand. "The feeling's mutual."

"I guess what I've noticed is that I like me better when I'm around you. I feel more confident, somehow. I know that you aren't going to laugh at me or make fun of me if I do or say the wrong thing."

"I feel the same way. It was a shock to discover how many degrees you *have* collected. That's pretty intimidating."

"But you weren't…intimidated, I mean. You saw me, the person, and not me, the wunderkind. You have no idea how normal that makes me feel."

He lifted her hand and placed it against his cheek. "I'm glad."

They rode along for several miles in silence before Joel asked, "What would you like to do tomorrow?"

"Surely I'll be able to go into work by then. Dr. Feldman should be returning from his vacation in a few days. I hope he's gotten as much out of his time off as I have mine. I feel like a new person."

According to Max, Feldman *was* working again, but at a laboratory that was known to very few people. Joel had stayed in touch with Max on a daily basis. The investigation into who was behind the attempt against Dr. Feldman and who had been following Melissa was progressing as rapidly as possible.

In the meantime, Joel knew that he was losing his objectivity on this case.

He'd never suspected that someone like Melissa Jordan could exist. Once he'd broken through her initial shyness, he found a delightful, humorous person with a tremendous capacity to enjoy life. Just being around her made him feel years younger.

She'd taught him a great deal about himself. Watching her learn to relax taught him how to do the same. Until he'd thought about needing to contact Max just now, Joel had been able to blot out the true reason they were together.

For the first time in his career, he wished that he could become the person he pretended to be, the person she thought he was. Instinctively, he made certain that they were not followed during their outings, but otherwise, he had allowed himself to become what he pretended to be, a friend who enjoyed her company.

Joel had never known another person in his life with whom he'd shared so much about himself. Instead of finding the idea that she knew so much about him threatening, he found it liberating.

He glanced over and saw that she had fallen asleep. She looked like a child in her jeans, heavy sweater and windbreaker, her hair pulled back into a high-swinging ponytail. She hadn't bothered with makeup. She didn't need to use any with her naturally dark eyebrows and lashes, her brilliant blue eyes and wind-flushed cheeks.

A couple of weeks ago, she had suggested that they not rush their friendship. So he had waited. However, he didn't intend to wait much longer. This woman had caused him to question some of his lifelong patterns. Joel no longer wanted to live a solitary life. He knew that now. It had taken only a few days of being around her for him to realize how much more there was to life than he had ever experienced.

He wanted to experience it all . . . with Melissa.


"How about a game of Scrabble after dinner?" Melissa asked him the following evening. They were in his apartment, a practice that had grown into a habit for them.

"I wouldn't stand a chance against you," he complained good-naturedly.

"Nonsense! Writers always know more words than anybody."

Joel considered his vocabulary adequate, but nothing unusual. Would she wonder about him if his skills were tested? They had been talking about going to a movie earlier, but decided against it. They hadn't rented any videos, and the television schedule hadn't appealed to them.

So what could they do to occupy themselves for the next few hours?

"Scrabble sounds fine."

"I'll go get my game and be right back." She'd dashed out the door before he could stop her.

Joel began to clear the table. What a darling she was. Watching the change in her over the past few weeks had been a revelation. He'd seen the exuberant young girl emerge from the serious scientist. Once she had gotten used to his sense of humor, she was quick with her own. He found it sad that such a vibrant woman had been hidden away for so long.

If spending this time together had done nothing else, it had helped her to open up to another person. Selfishly, Joel was glad he'd been the one to have witnessed the transformation.

"Here it is." She'd left his door slightly ajar so that she could get back in.

"How about having our coffee first?"

She disappeared into the kitchen and came out with two mugs filled with coffee. Joel walked over to her, took the mugs and set them on the coffee table in front of the sofa. Then he slipped his arms around her waist.

Her eyes widened. "What are you doing?"

He grinned. "With all those degrees, you still can't tell when a man's going to kiss you?"

Before she could find the words to reply, Joel proceeded to do just that. Melissa had grown accustomed to his affectionate gestures in the weeks she had known him, but this kiss was different somehow—more urgent, more possessive and much more intense.

When he picked her up and moved to the couch, she didn't resist. How could she? All he had to do was to touch her and her bones disintegrated. Somehow, she found herself lying on the couch beside him, responding to his touch.

When he finally paused, his voice shook. "I can't take much more of this, I'm afraid," he said hoarsely.

"Take what? Kissing me?" she managed to ask.

He groaned. "I want to do much more than kiss you."

"All right."

She felt him stiffen as he stared into her eyes. She met his gaze with a serene look. When he didn't say anything she sat up. "But wouldn't we be more comfortable in the bedroom?" She stood and held out her hand.

"Melissa?"

"Hmm?"

"Are you sure you want to do this?"

She nodded, unable to say the words.

Joel came to his feet. He knew he needed to keep a calm head. He was getting too wrapped up in his role-playing. He couldn't take advantage of the situation like this. He would have to tell her that—

A sudden explosion rocked the room.

# Chapter Four

The blast knocked them to the floor. Joel threw himself across Melissa, holding her close. Sounds of breaking glass and crackling fire filled the air along with the acrid scent of explosives.

Joel raised his head and looked around. Smoke billowed through a gaping hole that had once been the inside wall of his apartment. Long tentacles of flame filled what had been the hallway between their apartments. They could see directly into all that was left of Melissa's living room.

Even though he was dazed by the blast, Joel's training kicked in. Another explosion could occur at any moment. They had to get out of there. Fast.

Joel glanced down at Melissa, only now recognizing that he'd probably knocked the breath out of her when they fell. "Are you okay?"

She had the bewildered expression of a small child startled out of sleep, as though she didn't know whether to cry or demand an explanation. She blinked. "I think so," she offered in an uncertain voice.

Joel glanced around them. The fire was moving rapidly toward them. If they hadn't already been moving toward the hallway, the blast could have killed them. The couch where they'd been lying less than a minute ago was already on fire. He scrambled to his feet.

"We've got to get out of here. This place could go up any second."

He leaned down and grabbed her wrists, tugging her to her feet. As soon as she gained her balance, he pulled her behind him, running toward the bedroom.

Melissa glanced behind them. The living room was already a curtain of flames. She could no longer see into her apartment.

When she looked forward again, they were in Joel's bedroom. For the first time since the blast, she was aware of the panic beginning to build within her. They were trapped. How could they possibly get out of here?

Joel let go of her hand and sprinted toward his closet. He grabbed a couple of heavy parkas, reached into his bedside table and palmed the pistol hidden there. He turned, concealing the weapon in his hand and held out one of the jackets to her. "Put this on. You're going to need it."

While Melissa was occupied with pulling on the coat, Joel placed the pistol in the waist of his jeans at the small of his back, then shrugged into the other coat and gave the room a final glance. The building's fire alarm screamed in the still night air. Joel could hear the distant sound of sirens approaching.

He knew his first duty was to get Melissa out of there—to keep her safe. With that in mind, he grabbed her hand once again and headed toward the window.

"Where are we going? We're five stories up. We can't just—"

"We don't have a choice. Come on. There's a fire escape a couple of feet away." He had made certain there was an escape route in the apartment as soon as he moved in. He knew all the possible exits.

He shoved the window open and stepped through, then turned and helped Melissa over the windowsill. As soon as she was through, he lifted the hood of her coat and fastened it beneath her chin. She would be less identifiable in the dark with her bright mass of blond hair covered.

Joel took time to check out the area below them before starting their descent. He was counting on the fact that no one knew Melissa had been with him tonight. On the off chance she might have survived the initial blast, whoever had done this would be watching the windows on the other side of the building.

He hoped.

As soon as they reached the ground, he took her hand. "We've got to get away from here. The whole building could go up any time."

He moved into the darker shadows away from the building. After proceeding cautiously for a few feet, Joel began to sprint along a tree-lined jogging path that led into the surrounding park, still holding Melissa's hand.

Thank God she trusted him, he thought after a few minutes. He hadn't had time to explain anything to her. He was also thankful that she was in good physical shape. Every second counted for them at the moment. They needed to disappear—and fast.

Damn. He'd been lulled into a false sense of security these past few weeks. Surveillance had disappeared.

Either that or he was getting too old for this job because he hadn't spotted the perpetrators.

So how in the hell had they managed to get inside the building? They must have set off some sort of explosive in the hallway, which was the only thing that had saved him and Melissa. What if the damn thing had gone off when she'd run next door?

It didn't bear thinking about.

So now what were they going to do? He knew he'd have to come up with some fast alternative. Obviously, keeping an unobtrusive eye on his neighbor was no longer a viable option. It was time to jump to Plan B, whatever the hell that was.

The first thing he had to do was to get to a phone and let Max know what had happened, if he hadn't already been alerted.

Joel had gotten to know the surrounding neighborhood well, including the exact locations of the public telephones. The question was, which one would be the safest for them to use?

The convenience store. There were a couple of phones outside the building. He angled off the path without a pause.

Melissa began to fall behind, forcing him to slow his pace. She was panting when she asked, "Where are you going? Why are we running? Shouldn't we have stayed back there to find out what happened?"

Joel heard the short breaths that punctuated every other word. He continued moving away from the lighted area. His adrenaline had kicked in, something he was familiar with. Without looking around at her, he said, "Has it occurred to you that somebody just tried to kill you? Do you want to hang around and give them another chance?"

She stopped dead in her tracks so that Joel was forced to stop and look at her. With his hands on his hips, he drew deep breaths of cold air into his lungs.

"Me?" She stared at him as though convinced he'd lost his mind. "Why would anybody want to kill *me?*" She glanced around them and shivered. "That explosion was an accident! The fire department is going to have some questions. We need to go back. If we aren't there, everyone will think we were killed!"

He shook his head. "Melissa, think about it for a moment. What sort of accident would cause an explosion like that? Someone was making sure that those apartments were destroyed, with us in them. Do you honestly want to go back and take a chance on somebody trying to finish the job?"

Her mind was whirling with confused thoughts. Everything was happening too fast. She couldn't think straight. "I don't understand any of this." She brushed the hood away from her face. "If we'd still been on the couch..." Her voice trailed off.

"I know."

She shuddered, wrapping her arms around her own waist. "I couldn't believe what was happening. It all took place so fast." She looked up at him. "If you hadn't gotten us out of there, we could have died."

"It's amazing how the need for self-preservation can motivate a person, isn't it?" He purposely kept his voice light, but he wrapped his arms around her and held her close. He could still feel her shaking. And why not? His heart was going fast enough to compete with a marathon runner.

He glanced around them. They were still near the jogging path that ran through the park near their apartment building. If someone decided to scout around, they could still be spotted.

"Honey, we need to find a phone. We've got to figure out where we're going to stay." He kissed the end of her nose. "I don't know about you, but I don't want to have to sleep in the park tonight."

She buried her face in his neck and clung to him. "Joel?"

"Hmm."

"Why did you suggest that someone is trying to harm me? I'm nobody important." She raised her head so that she could see his face. "Maybe what happened was meant for you."

"Possibly, but I rather doubt it. None of the editors I know have resorted to bombs to signify their rejection of my work." He took her hand and led her into the trees. "Let's get out of here, okay? I'm not in the mood to run into a mugger out here, either."

"But where can we go?"

At least she began to jog along beside him as he stepped up the pace once again, Joel noticed with a sense of relief. "I thought I'd call a friend to see if he could suggest a place for us to stay." Trying to stave off any arguments, he said, "I don't know about you, but I'd prefer not to go to a hotel, if we can find an alternative."

She didn't say anything and Joel felt a sense of relief that she hadn't argued with him. Now that the immediate danger was past, he could no longer dismiss what had been taking place at the time of the explosion. Another few minutes and they would have been in bed!

For a brief moment, Joel allowed himself to focus on the memory of her pressed against him, his mouth on hers. He could feel her softness, catch the tantalizing scent of her light perfume. Actually, nothing less than an explosion would have stopped him from making love to her tonight.

By the time they reached a well-lighted part of the park, they were both breathing hard. Joel shook his head, disgusted that their flight had come close to winding him. He paused, placing his hand lightly on her upper arm.

"What's wrong?"

Damn, but she was sensitive to his moods. He would have to be careful not to needlessly alarm her. He draped his arm across her shoulders. "Nothing. I just don't see any need to race across the street as though we're being chased by the hounds of hell."

The look she gave him was made up of puzzled amusement. "But you saw nothing wrong with our headlong rush through the park, I take it."

"Hell, no. There's no telling who's lurking in the bushes at this time of night."

Melissa looked back at the way they had come and shivered. In an attempt to lighten the mood, she smiled at him and said, "My hero."

He leaned over so that he could touch his nose to hers. His smile flashed white in his tanned face. "And don't you forget it."

By the time they entered the small store, they looked like any other couple out for a brisk walk on a cold night.

"Why don't you get us something to drink while I make my call?" He glanced around at the brightly lit store. She would be safe inside while he used the phone. The front wall of the building was made up of glass, which gave him visual access to her.

"What do you want to drink?"

"Surprise me."

Her mischievous smile managed to do just that. He could still see the shock in her face, and yet she was determinedly teasing him in an effort to overcome her fears. Joel had an absurd impulse to hug her to him, to promise her that she would be safe. Instead, he gave her a mock salute and walked back into the cold night air.

He pulled a handful of change out of his pocket, selected a coin and dialed the number. The call was answered on the first ring.

"Yeah. It's me," he said before the other man spoke.

"Joel! Where are you? Is Dr. Jordan all right?"

So Max had already learned of the explosion. "She's with me," he replied, and he gave Max their location. "Looks like we're going to have to look at some alternatives to the original plan."

He could hear the relief in Max's voice. "I'll admit to being shaken when the report came in. What happened?"

"I don't know. We'd finished with dinner and were having coffee when all hell broke loose. Have you heard how bad the damage was?"

"They're still battling the blaze. Authorities on the scene don't see much chance of saving the building." There was a brief pause before he added in a low voice, "They could have gotten both of you with this one, Kramer."

"Yeah, I know. I think we'd better tell her what's going on, don't you?"

"Not necessarily. Why cause her more alarm?"

"Are you kidding? What's more alarming than having your home blown into tiny particles?"

"What I mean is, there's no reason to let her know she's the target of a possible assassination."

"Come on, Max! She's no dummy. I've got to tell her something. How in the hell am I going to convince her to hide away with me somewhere if I don't tell her the truth?"

Max chuckled. "How about using your charm?"

"Very funny."

"I'm serious. Use that charm of yours and convince her the two of you could enjoy going away together."

"As a matter of fact, we've been enjoying our day trips—to the point where she's mentioned the possibility of a vacation next summer. But we're talking about now."

"Where does she want to go on vacation?"

"I'm not sure. She said something about a friend having a place in the Virgin Islands that she keeps being invited to share."

"Virgin Islands. That might be a good idea. Do you think you could convince her to go now?"

"Without telling her why? No. No, I don't. Look, Max, Melissa is a strong, courageous woman. I don't see any reason to keep her in the dark on this one. Full knowledge might be the extra edge that keeps her alive."

"You don't think you can protect her?"

"I didn't say that."

"Once you get her away from here for a few days, there'll be no reason to tell her. We expect to be in a position to move on this one shortly. Surely you can manage to take care of her that long without discussing what's going on with her."

"And if I can't? Are you willing to take the risk, Max? Because I'm telling you right now, I'm not."

Max didn't answer just then. After a long moment of silence, he finally said, "Don't blow your cover, Kramer. That's an order. If you can tell her anything without explaining who you are, then do it. Otherwise, no.''

In all his years at this job, Joel had never come close to stepping out of his assigned role. Max was right. He couldn't afford to do so now. Somehow, he had to continue to be a writer as far as Melissa was concerned.

''If the friend isn't willing to cooperate, do you have any other suggestions for where we could go?''

''The beach house is available.''

''Max, it's wintertime, in case you hadn't noticed.''

''So? Few people would be hanging around this time of the year. Anyone around would be suspect. I can also put more men on the case without her seeing them.''

''We'll go that route if we have to. I'll let you know. But if I have to head for a beach, I'd prefer the Caribbean.''

''Yeah, wouldn't we all?''

He glanced up and saw Melissa at the counter paying for two cups of coffee.

''Look, I've gotta go. She'll be here in a moment.''

''Good luck. And keep in touch. Who knows, I might have a *real* job for you in a few days. Try not to get too bored.''

''I'll try to remember that,'' Joel drawled before putting the receiver down and turning to the approaching woman.

''Here you are.'' She handed him one of the containers.

''Thanks.''

''You didn't look too happy talking with your friend just now,'' she offered with a tentative smile. ''Is there some problem?''

''Yes and no,'' Joel prevaricated. ''I guess I'm just upset. My friend had picked up the news of the explosion on his police scanner," he improvised. "The whole building has gone up, although the people on the other floors were evacuated without much danger. It's mass confusion there. The best thing we can do is stay away."

Melissa shivered. "We're lucky to be alive."

He glanced around at the darkened street and slowly moved Melissa and himself into the deeper shadows at the side of the building. "Do you remember talking about your friend's place in the Islands?"

His sudden change of subject caused Melissa to look at him in surprise. "Yes, why?"

"I was just thinking about how nice it would be to get away from this cold weather for a few days. I don't suppose she'd be willing to let us use her place since we're temporarily homeless these days."

Homeless. Her mind hadn't fully comprehended all that had happened to her tonight. Her home—all of her possessions—everything was gone. All she had left was what she wore. Not even that, she amended, looking at the coat Joel had loaned her.

"Melissa?"

She hadn't realized that tears were rolling down her cheeks until Joel set his coffee on the ledge by the telephone, cupped her face in his hands and gently brushed the tears away with his thumbs.

"Don't cry, love. Please don't cry. We'll work something out, okay? If you don't want to ask her, we can go somewhere else. My friend has a place on the coast of North Carolina. It's just a summer cottage, but it might be fun to go over there for a couple of days." He leaned down and brushed his lips across her mouth. "We've both been through quite a shock. I think it would do us both good to get away from everything." He held her close to his body. "Let's go somewhere safe and give the police a chance to investigate what happened."

How could she possibly think straight at the moment? She closed her eyes, and he lightly kissed each eyelid, causing them to quiver in reaction to his touch.

"Let me look after you, Melissa. Please."

Joel forgot the role he was supposed to be playing. He forgot everything except the need to stay with this woman and to keep her safe from harm. She intrigued him like no other woman ever had. She was such a mixture of innocence and knowledge, of fierce independence and gentle yielding. He felt as though his heart had paused in its rhythmic beat and the air refused to move in his lungs while he waited for her answer.

"Nothing like this has ever happened to me before," she managed to say in a moment.

"All right. Let's look at your options...at both our options. We don't have a place to stay. Luckily for you, we still haven't gotten your car, so it wasn't in the garage tonight, but mine was, so at the moment, we're without transportation. We each have friends with summer places. We could go to North Carolina or fly down to Miami and go to the Virgin islands, if you think your friend wouldn't mind."

"I don't think she'd mind. She's always told me to feel free to use it whenever I could."

"Would you mind if I went with you?"

Her gaze met his. "Is that what you want?"

He nodded. "Very much."

Melissa stood in the circle of his arms, trying to come to grips with the unexpected events during the past few hours. Her job came first, of course, but the building was closed for the rest of the week. Her home had been destroyed and she had no place to stay. Joel's suggestion made a lot of sense. He'd made it clear that she wouldn't have to be alone, not if she didn't want to be.

Was it just a few weeks ago when she was stumbling over how to deal with Joel's invitation to spend a vacation together? Hadn't she learned anything during these past few weeks? Hadn't she learned how to break the myriad rules that governed her life? *Live a little,* she reminded herself. *Enjoy the joys of spontaneity. Be outrageous for the first time in your life.*

She gave Joel a tremulous smile. "I'll call Karen right now."

## Chapter Five

Melissa wearily opened her eyes and looked around the Miami airport terminal. At two o'clock in the morning, very few people were there. She located Joel casually leaning against a counter, chatting with an airline employee—a female employee who looked as though she was thoroughly enjoying the attention.

Melissa closed her eyes, wishing she could stretch out for a few moments of rest. Three short hours ago, the idea of flying to an island in the sun had had all the earmarks of an exciting adventure. Now all that could arouse her interest was a place to sleep. Obviously, she was not the stuff that adventurers were made out of.

Karen had been delighted to hear from her, and even more delighted to give her directions to her vacation cottage. Melissa had handed the phone to Joel at that point, which had created a barrage of questions when he'd returned the receiver to Melissa. She knew she'd have a great deal of explaining to do when they returned because Karen had only laughed at Melissa's explanation that she and Joel were friends who happened to need a place to stay for a few days.

Melissa could understand Karen's doubts because she was developing more than a few herself as each hour passed. She hadn't really thought about how much of her time had been taken up with Joel recently and how necessary he'd become to her. Their friendship had grown steadily and naturally. It was only when she heard Karen's astonishment and rapid-fire questions that Melissa realized how out of character her recent behavior had been.

"Melissa?"

Joel's distinctive voice seemed to touch every part of her. She would recognize it anywhere. She opened her eyes and found him crouched beside her knees, a concerned expression on her face.

She smiled at him and absently brushed his hair off his forehead.

"Are you okay?" he asked.

She nodded. "Just tired."

"The first flight out of here won't be for another three hours. If you want, we could check into one of the hotels nearby. We don't have to take an early flight, for that matter."

"It doesn't matter to me. Whatever you want to do."

Joel glanced around the terminal. He felt very exposed there. "I think we both need some sleep. Since this is a vacation, there's no reason to arrive exhausted." He stood and pulled her to her feet. "Let's go get horizontal."

She grinned. "What a romantic offer. How could I possibly refuse!"

He recalled what had occurred immediately prior to the explosion. He'd come so close to making a major mistake. He knew better than to get personally involved, and yet he also knew that he couldn't ignore what was happening between the two of them. *Be a pro,* he reminded himself. He could certainly choose not to allow a physical relationship with Melissa to further complicate matters.

He draped his arm over her shoulders and led her away from the waiting area and toward the exit doors. He nodded to the airline employee when she gave him a wave, but continued walking. "We can hop a shuttle bus to the nearest hotel, check in, get some sleep, then head south tomorrow."

She nodded, too tired to care.

By the time they arrived at the hotel and had been given the key, Melissa looked almost comatose to Joel. She hadn't blinked when he asked for one room with double beds. There was no way he was going to let her out of his sight, not after what had happened, and he was grateful that she hadn't argued.

He found their room and opened the door. She immediately went to one of the beds and sat down. She still carried his parka clutched to her chest. Her hair was tangled and fell in abandoned waves around her face. Her eyes looked swollen from lack of sleep.

"Do you want to take a shower?"

She nodded but didn't move.

"Or would you rather wait until morning?"

She nodded once again.

He shook his head. She'd had a very tough night and had held up very well. He walked over to her and gently removed the coat from her arms, then knelt and untied her sneakers. Reaching around her, he tugged at the covers, lifted her slightly so that he could pull them back, then gently lowered her head onto the pillow. She didn't stir when he lifted her legs and tucked them under the covers.

Joel went into the bathroom and turned on the shower. As soon as he'd stripped out of his clothes, placing his pistol on top of them, he stepped beneath the soothing spray.

Whenever he flew commercially, he contacted the security force of each airline, showed his special ID and checked his pistol with them. It had all been done unobtrusively. He'd explained his purpose for carrying it and had shown his permit.

So far, so good. One more flight, a short boat ride to the small island where they were going, and he would have her safe.

Her friend Karen had sounded as though she wanted to ask a hundred questions, but she had refrained. Instead, her directions had been clear and concise. He grinned. He had a hunch that Melissa would have some explaining to do the next time she and Karen spoke.

He sighed, turning beneath the spray so that the hot water hit his neck and shoulder muscles. The needlelike spray felt as though it were kneading the tense muscles. Joel consciously worked to relax so that he could sleep. He needed to stay alert and he couldn't do that without some much-needed rest. No one had shown any interest in them while they were at the airport, nor had anyone followed them to the hotel. For a few hours, at least, he could relax his guard.

By the time he turned off the water and toweled himself dry, he was ready to hit the sack. He tied the towel around his waist, gathered up his clothes and quietly entered the bedroom.

Melissa hadn't moved.

He placed the pistol on the floor beside his bed, removed the towel and slipped between the covers. He couldn't remember when a bed had felt so good to him. Within minutes he was asleep.

When Melissa opened her eyes several hours later, she had no idea where she was. A thin strip of light from the window where the drapes did not quite meet was the only illumination in the room.

The only thing she was certain of was that she wasn't at home. Home. Memories began to impinge on her consciousness. Being with Joel . . . the explosion . . . running through the night . . . calling Karen . . . flying south . . . sitting in the airport . . . . But she didn't remember this room.

She raised up on one elbow and looked around. She could barely see the other bed in the shadowed room, could barely make out the outline of someone sleeping there.

Joel. He lay on his stomach, his head burrowed into the pillow, facing away from her. The covers lay draped around his waist. She had never seen him without a shirt before.

If the explosion hadn't occurred when it did, she would have seen much more than his bare chest. She could feel her face flame at the thought. Was the explosion an omen of sorts? It had certainly interrupted what seemed to be inevitable between her and Joel.

She had never felt so close to another person before, not even her parents. It hadn't been their fault that they hadn't been affectionate or demonstrative, and Melissa hadn't missed what she'd never had. However, after being around Joel, she'd discovered the joys of touching—which he seemed to do with ease—and hugging—another thing that seemed to come naturally to him. And his kisses . . . would she ever get enough of them?

Melissa quietly slid from the bed and tiptoed into the bathroom. She glanced into the mirror and cringed, wondering what she was going to do with her hair.

After quickly removing her clothes, she stepped into the shower. Thank God the hotel furnished complimentary shampoo for people like her, who hadn't brought any. She had escaped with only what she had been wearing.

Joel had suggested that they wait until today to shop for clothes. She was at a loss to know where to start trying to replace what had been lost in the explosion. Even her purse and all her identification was gone. Joel had explained on the flight from D.C. to Miami that everything could be replaced. It would just take time. In the meantime, he would pay for whatever she needed, since his wallet had been in his pocket when the explosion occurred.

For now, she would have to put on her sweater and jeans once again. The thought of wearing what she'd worn yesterday didn't thrill her, but she knew she was lucky to have that, under the circumstances. She was lucky to be alive.

What if she *had* been killed? She would have died without ever having experienced much. It was as though she'd been given a second chance to discover life. This time, she intended to open her eyes to everything around her.

By the time she finished her shower and dressed, Melissa discovered that her stomach was growling. She couldn't remember the last time she'd eaten, but she knew she was going to need something soon.

She opened the door to the bedroom and found Joel sitting on the side of the bed with the sheets draped decorously around him.

"Good morning," she said with a smile.

"You okay?" he asked, studying her intently.

"Of course. Why wouldn't I be?"

"I was worried about you last night. I think we pushed you past your limits."

"Well, you have to admit we had a full day yesterday."

"Agreed."

"Joel, do you by any chance have a comb I could use?"

He grinned at her earnest expression. "Is that all it will take to make you content?"

"Well, a comb and some breakfast would go a long way toward that end."

He leaned over and picked up his pants, searched through them and handed her a small pocket comb.

"Thanks." She disappeared into the bathroom.

As soon as the door closed, he stood and stepped into his pants. He'd had a scare when he awakened and saw her bed empty. For a brief moment, he'd been afraid that somehow, someone had come in and—

But then he'd heard a soft sound in the bathroom and realized where she was. If he didn't watch it, he would become downright paranoid. He'd never been responsible for another person before. It felt much different from just looking after himself. He wondered if that feeling of responsibility was what a parent felt. If so, he wasn't sure he could live with it on a daily basis. His nerves were already on edge, and he and Melissa had only been on the move for about twelve hours.

By the time she came out of the bathroom with her hair combed, but damp, Joel was dressed.

"Let's go get something to eat, do some shopping and grab a plane heading south," he suggested with a grin.

She nodded. "Sounds great."

It was early evening by the time they approached the small cottage that Karen had carefully described. They had already taken a plane and a boat, and were now in a taxi that had enjoyed its prime around the Second World War.

Melissa sat in isolated splendor in the back seat while Joel chatted with the driver, asking about sailboat rentals, scuba-diving equipment, the best places to eat and other general information.

What surprised her was that he was carrying on the conversation in Spanish.

"I didn't know they spoke Spanish in the Virgin Islands," she said, not realizing she'd spoken her thoughts until Joel looked around at her.

"It isn't the native language, if that's what you mean," he said. "Carlos is from Puerto Rico."

"Oh. I didn't know you spoke Spanish."

He shrugged. "One of the ranch hands was from Mexico. It's an easy language to pick up. I learned it before I was old enough to consider languages difficult."

The car slowed and turned onto a path that looked barely wide enough for a vehicle. After following the trail for a few hundred yards, the car pulled into a clearing, and Joel and Melissa saw the house for the first time.

Although small, it looked well built, as though it could withstand the sudden storms that periodically originated in that area.

Joel looked at her. "I believe this is Karen's place."

She nodded, seeing a small carved wooden sign with the family name on it near the door. "Yes." She couldn't take it all in—the flowering shrubs, the tropical scented air, the lush greenness all around. "Oh, Joel, this is beautiful."

He got out of the car and opened the door. After helping her out, he grabbed the two bags they'd bought that morning to carry their other purchases.

After paying off the driver and arranging for him to pick them up the next day so that they could explore the harbor town, Joel turned toward the house.

"Shall we go in?"

Melissa was almost afraid to move. She felt as though she was under some island magical spell and she didn't want to spoil the sensation. *Don't be silly,* she reminded herself. *Now you understand why Karen has tried to get you to come down here before.*

She climbed the steps to the wide porch that encircled the house. The key was where Karen had told them it would be, and Melissa quickly opened the door, holding it open so that Joel could step through with their bags.

Each room looked out onto the beach. Melissa walked to the sliding doors, unlocked them and stepped outside.

"I've never seen anything like this before."

Joel joined her at the railing. "Now this is my idea of winter weather." He stared down the stairs. "Let's go exploring."

The beach was in a small cove that ended at a cluster of rocks. After they clambered to the top, they could see the jungle vegetation had taken over the inlet next to the one they had come from. The foliage grew to within a couple of feet of the water.

Melissa turned and looked back toward the house. The sun was beginning to set, and the scene looked like something from a travel magazine or postcard—the palm trees were silhouetted against a dark blue sky with rays of pink and light blue projected across it. The sand looked as though it had been bleached white.

"I feel as though I'm going to wake up any moment," she whispered. "This can't be real."

"I'm glad you suggested coming down here."

"Oh, me, too."

This was paradise. There was no doubt in Melissa's mind. She watched the lazy waves wash up on the shore, trimming it with lacy foam.

Melissa had always dealt in facts, figures and science; in what could be analyzed, processed and proven. Nothing in her experience had prepared her for the sheer magic of nature in all of her bountiful splendor.

Melissa turned to Joel and found that he was watching her. "I've never seen anything so wonderful," she said softly.

"Neither have I," he replied, his gaze never leaving her face.

She turned away, unable to handle the emotion that washed over her at the look on his face. She began to clamber down the pile of rocks. As soon as she reached the sand, she slipped off her sneakers and walked to the edge of the water. She touched it with her toe. "It's so warm," she marveled, looking around at him.

He stood watching her, his hands in his pockets. "Yes."

"I never realized. I guess I'm used to the water in New England."

He glanced at the sky. "We'd better get back to the house. Darkness comes quickly in the tropics."

Melissa obligingly walked to where he was standing. She held a shoe in each hand. He took one from her so that he could hold her hand, and they walked back to the house in silence.

As soon as they reached the house, they looked through each room. Melissa felt no sense of unease while they chose which bedroom each would use. Then they went into the kitchen to check the supplies.

"We'll pick up fresh food when we go into town tomorrow. But there's enough canned goods here to feed us tonight," Joel pointed out.

Melissa yawned and hastily covered her mouth with her hand.

"It's all that fresh air," Joel pointed out.

"That must be it. It can't be the company."

He looked at her with raised eyebrows. "I certainly hope not, at least not quite so early in our vacation."

"We can't stay long, you know," she said quietly.

"Yes. I know."

"It's going to be difficult trying to make insurance claims, finding a new place to live when we return."

"That's true, but for the next few days, let's enjoy where we are. Let's just live in the moment... forget the past and the future. After all, this is the only time that we have any control over."

She nodded. "Then I intend to enjoy every second." She looked at the cans they had set out on the counter. "As soon as we get this meal put together, I'm going to bed. There's so much to do, I'm not sure what I want to do first."

Joel took her hands and placed them on his chest. "Thank you for inviting me here."

"It wouldn't be the same without you. I'm glad you suggested getting away."

He leaned down and kissed her softly on the lips. "Meeting you has been the most magical experience I've had since I was a child. I'm still not sure you're real."

She slipped her arms around his neck. "I feel exactly the same way." When she kissed him, she allowed all of her emotions full rein. Her Big Adventure had started. She would never again have such a golden opportunity to experience life.

Melissa had every intention of making the most of it.

## Chapter Six

Bright sunlight streamed through the slats covering Melissa's bedroom windows when she first opened her eyes. The warmth of the room had caused her to kick off her covers the night before. For a few blissful moments, Melissa closed her eyes once again and lay there, content to drift in that delicious time somewhere between dreams and reality.

She was aware of the comfortable bed, the warm air, the soft sounds of the waves nearby and the slight rustle of the breeze through the broad-leaved plants next to the porch. Eventually she could no longer resist peeking once more at the view she'd first discovered when they arrived.

She climbed out of bed and padded barefoot to the window. Bright green foliage and a lush carpet of grass edged the white sand. She could not resist the temptation to go outside. Ignoring the fact that she was wearing only an oversize T-shirt, Melissa pushed open the slatted door beside the window and stepped outside. There was no resisting the compelling pull of the sun, the sand and the sea.

She felt as though she were the only one in this colorful paradise. When she reached the shoreline, she looked up and down the gracefully curving beach but saw no one. Nothing marred the pristine freshness. This must have been how it looked on the day of Creation.

Melissa felt an ache in her chest that seemed to grow and fill her with the pain of unexpressed emotion. She wanted to laugh, to cry, to leap into the air. She wanted to throw her arms in the air and sing praises.

When a curl of a wave brushed lightly across her toes, she looked down and laughed. She threw her arms wide and twirled in a circle, causing the shallow wave to splash against her bare legs. The warm salt water felt like silk, and she waded outward, going up on her toes as the waves lapped around her legs. One audacious wave welled up, striking her at the waist and soaking her nightshirt. She retaliated by diving into its midst. *This must be how a dolphin feels swimming in the water,* she decided when she surfaced, shoving her hair away from her face and allowing it to stream down her back. She felt free to experience the elements.

When she grew breathless and her muscles were in a state of relaxed tiredness, she waded to shore, wringing the water from her hair.

She'd worked up an appetite, one she had every intention of appeasing as soon as possible. With a light step, she retraced her earlier route, let herself into her bedroom and walked into the adjoining bathroom, where she peeled off the sodden nightshirt and climbed into the shower.

Melissa Jordan's day had been jubilantly launched.

* * *

Joel stood looking out the sliding glass doors off the living area. Watching Melissa run, jump and frolic in the water had caused a lump to form in his throat. She'd been like a small child who had just discovered how to play in the ocean. And yet . . . and yet, when she returned to the house, she had been all woman: alluring, tempting and very desirable.

Her wet garment clung to her body, providing little cover. She looked like a water nymph, lightly dancing up the pathway, a part of nature that might disappear before his eyes.

He could feel his heart racing in his chest. What he had just witnessed had affected him to such a degree that he felt physically weak.

When had this woman become so important to him? When had being around her become more than a job . . . had, instead, become a need to last a lifetime? He tried to rationalize his feelings. He understood that the situation was unusual, the circumstances far from normal. None of that mattered.

He loved her. He had loved her probably from the very first—if he had only recognized it. But how could he have identified such an overwhelming emotion that he'd never before experienced. His feelings had grown daily until he could no longer ignore or mistake what he was feeling.

He wished to hell he knew what to do about it.

"Good morning! Isn't it a beautiful day?"

He hadn't heard her enter the room. He swung away from the view and looked at her. She'd changed into a pair of shorts and a summer blouse. Her hair hung in a single braid, her feet were bare.

She looked adorable.

"Did you enjoy your swim?"

For a moment, she looked surprised, then she laughed. "Yes, I did. Very much. You must have thought I'd lost my mind out there."

"Not at all. If anything, I was envying you."

"You should have joined me."

"I don't think that would have been a good idea."

"Why?"

He glanced at his watch. "We might have missed our ride to town. It's almost time."

"Oh! I had no idea it was that late." She turned away. "I'll get my purse. Even without any money, I feel more comfortable carrying it."

A horn honked outside.

"There he is. I'll be right there," she said, and disappeared down the hallway.

They were both in the back seat of the taxi, and on the way to town when Melissa suddenly gasped and said, "Joel!"

"What is it?"

Her hand had flown to her mouth. "Oh, Joel! I just remembered your manuscript. With everything that's happened, I had forgotten all that you've lost, as well. Just think of all that work gone."

He felt a pang of guilt at her obvious concern.

"It isn't the end of the world, I guess. I remember most of my references. I should be able to reconstruct what I've done."

She touched his hand. "It's still a loss that you haven't dwelled on in your efforts to help me. I know how I'd feel if all the work I'd produced over the past months was destroyed."

He didn't know what to say, so he remained quiet. Damn. He hated the fact that she saw him as some heroic personage suffering in silence. He wished he didn't have to go through with this charade, but could tell her the truth about himself.

Another shock to his system. Never before had he been willing to share who he was with another person. Now, when he'd met the woman who meant the world to him, he couldn't tell her. At least, not right now. Just as soon as Max gave him the all-clear sign, he'd explain to Melissa who he was and what he did for a living.

For now, he'd just have to learn patience.

He turned his hand, catching hers, and slipped his fingers through hers. "At the moment, all I want to do is to enjoy our tropical island."

She squeezed his hand. "Me, too."


Hours later, Joel wondered if Melissa had any idea of the severe tests she was forcing him to face with regard to his self-control. Didn't she have any idea how irresistible she looked in the bikini she'd finally chosen...or the strapless sundress that showed off her soft shoulders and contrasted so attractively with her hair.

The shorts and halter tops she'd chosen revealed her long, shapely legs and tantalizing cleavage.

How was he going to spend any time with Melissa in this romantic paradise without making love to her? And if he did, wouldn't he be taking advantage of the peculiar circumstances that had brought them together?

They were seated at one of the local restaurants, and he kept gazing out over the water, trying to find the strength to leave her alone.

"Joel?"

He removed his gaze from the harbor and focused on her. "Hmm?"

"You're thinking about your manuscript, aren't you?"

"Why do you ask?"

"I just wondered. Every so often, you get a certain expression on your face, as though you're working out some sort of complex problem in your mind. It must be tough knowing how much effort it's going to take to replace what you lost."

He glanced down at the table, hating the thought of making up yet another lie. Instead, he chose to say, "I'm sorry. I know I'm not being very good company at the moment."

She touched his hand that rested on the table. "You don't owe me an apology. I understand what you're feeling."

"Do you?"

She nodded. "No matter how much I try to pretend, I still haven't faced the reality of all that's happened. It's hard to look at the fact that I have nothing left, that when I return, I've got to start all over." They were quiet for several minutes before she spoke again. "I just wish I could make some sense of it all." She cocked her head slightly, meeting his gaze. "Do you have some enemies that might be after you?"

"*Me!* What makes you think that bombing had anything to do with me?"

"Because nothing else makes any sense. If it had been a random bombing of the entire building, whoever did it wouldn't have placed it on our floor. Since it was placed there, they could have been after only one of us." She took another sip of her drink. "I don't know what you've been doing in the way of research, but could it be possible that you offended someone somewhere? Where were you before you moved to Virginia?"

Joel thought of his last assignment. Was it possible that . . . No. Of course not. He knew exactly why the bomb had been set. For the same reason that Peter Feldman had been run off the road. The problem was that he couldn't give Melissa that necessary tidbit of information.

Sometimes the agency's need for secrecy became absurd. His job would be so much more simple if he could just explain to her what was going on. There were times when the old need-to-know policy could be a real pain in the posterior.

This was one of them.

"Aren't you going to tell me?"

"Tell you what?"

She dropped her gaze for a moment, wishing that she had never started this conversation. "Where you were before you moved here."

He had no choice but to lie. "Texas. I was doing some research in south Texas." Actually, he'd been flown into Brownsville via Mexico when they'd smuggled him out of Central America.

"Can you think of anyone down there who might have been offended by what you were doing?"

He tried not to react to the innocent question, even though it triggered a myriad of memories. Yes, he could think of a few people who hated his guts, all right.

"Not really, no."

She looked disappointed.

"How about you?" he asked in an effort to get her mind off him. "Do you have any enemies?"

Her laughter rang in the room. "I'm afraid not. My life is much too boring to have accumulated anything so exciting."

"What about your work?"

She sobered, obviously considering his question. After a few moments, she shook her head. "I love my work, but it's far from exciting. At least, most of the time."

"You've never told me exactly what you do."

She smiled. "It's classified."

"No kidding. You work for the government?"

"No. It's a private company, but you know how competitive private industry is. Always afraid of industrial spies." She eyed him with mock suspicion. "For all I know, you could be an industrial spy worming your way into my confidence to learn everything I know."

He grinned. "So how am I doing?"

She patted his hand. "I'd look for another line of work if I were you."

"Oh, really?"

She nodded. "You're too open and honest. You're not the type to harbor deep, dark secrets. You're very easy to read, as a matter of fact."

"You don't say. So tell me what I'm thinking at this moment."

She grinned. "I didn't say I could read minds. I just said that you were easy to read."

He slouched back in his chair and stared at her. "Okay. So read me."

She sobered and stared at him for a moment. "All right," she said with a nod. "You don't like working for another person because you don't take orders well. You have a deep-seated desire to be independent, to be free from all restraints and routines. You're easily bored, partly because of your intelligence and strong need to be intellectually stimulated."

Alarms rang inside Joel's head. He sat up abruptly. He felt the same way he'd felt when he read that absurd piece about the Gemini man; he resented the fact that she had been able to describe him so accurately.

"What are you, some kind of witch?" he growled.

"Was I close?"

"Close enough." He took a drink from his neglected glass of rum punch. Setting the glass back down, he responded, "You sound like one of those star gazers."

She laughed, sounding pleased. "I do, don't I?" She reached across the table and took his hand. In a pseudo-solemn tone, she asked, "What is your sun sign, Signore?"

He studied her for a moment before he grinned. "I'll tell mine if you'll tell yours."

"I'm a Libra."

"Hmm...whatever that is." He shrugged. "I'm supposedly a Gemini."

"So you're Joel, the Gemini man," she pointed out with a grin which faded into a look of bemusement. "Do you find me easy to read?"

"Perhaps."

"OK, so read me," she invited with a mischievous smile.

He remembered the information that Feldman had given him about her, then discarded it. Nothing he'd been told described the woman he'd gotten to know over the past few weeks.

"You sure you want me to do this?" he asked.

Her eyes reflected her shyness but she nodded gamely.

He was quiet for a few moments, gazing at her intently. Then in a low voice, he began to speak. "You have a very becoming blush that appears at the most intriguing moments—such as now—that makes me want to know what thoughts are running around in that head of yours." He paused and raised one eyebrow. "Shall I go on?"

Even though her cheeks glowed, she nodded.

"Let's see, then. You're very conscientious in your work, very dedicated. You don't go out very often and seem to enjoy your own company. You have the greatest pair of legs I've seen this side of the Rockettes in Rocke-feller Center. You have eyes that haunt my sleep, a smile that melts my heart and a mouth that continues to lure me into indiscretions that could get me into very serious trouble.''

Her face matched the color of the setting sun. ''Aren't you being a little personal?''

''Weren't you?''

''Not in the same way. I didn't talk about your physical appearance and how it affects me.''

He waved his hand. ''Feel free,'' he offered expansively.

She clasped her hands in front of her. With her eyes on her hands, she muttered, ''I don't think that's a very good idea.''

''Why? Afraid you'll blush? Don't worry about it. I'm used to you changing colors. It's one of your most charming characteristics.''

She didn't reply, but Joel was determined not to let her off the hook. While he waited, he signaled the bartender to bring them another round of the island's specialty drink. The alcoholic content made Long Island Tea seem like a bland after-dinner drink by comparison.

They sat in silence and watched the sun set. When the waiter brought their drinks Joel suggested he bring them something from the kitchen, as well.

During their meal, Melissa sighed and finally spoke. ''All right. I'm not sure why we're doing this, but here goes.'' She closed her eyes for a moment, then took a healthy sip from her very potent drink. As though she were afraid that she wouldn't be able to say it unless she got it out quickly, Melissa began to speak in a low, hurried voice.

"You have a way of walking that puts me in mind of a dancer—or maybe a feline...like a jungle cat stalking its prey. You move silently with a conscious intent that I find captivating. When you walk toward me like that, I find that I can't move. I just wait to see what you're going to do." She paused for breath, grabbed her glass and took another large swallow. "You have an air of confidence about you that intrigues and attracts me." She forced herself to meet his gaze. "I find you one of the most attractive men I've ever been around so that I don't know how to hide my reaction to you. I feel like a gawky adolescent with my first crush."

Joel had become instantly aroused from her very first words. He sat there listening to her, reminding himself that he had teased her into disclosing what was obviously a very personal revelation.

She had no sooner finished speaking than he was reaching for his wallet. He threw some bills on the table, stood and held out his hand. "Let's get out of here. Otherwise, I'm going to embarrass both of us."

# *Chapter Seven*

Within minutes of leaving the small restaurant, they were by the harbor. The cool breeze helped Joel to gain some control over his reaction to her words.

When had he ever had anyone be so honest with him? She had no artifice or shield to protect herself. He could hurt this woman badly, and that was the last thing he wanted.

He loved her. Like it or not, convenient or not, ethical or not, he was in love with Dr. Melissa Jordan. What in the hell was he going to do?

They reached the end of the boardwalk and took the stairs down to the sand-covered beach. The stars were the only light they had besides the reflected lights from the small town.

"Melissa?"

"Hmm?"

"I need to tell you something."

She stared up at him through the heavy shadows around them.

"All right."

He turned and took her into his arms and held her close, so close that he could feel her heart beating in her chest, could feel the gentle rise and fall of her breasts as she breathed. "Melissa, I lied to you."

She pulled her head away from his shoulder and stared up at him. "What do you mean?"

"Do you remember when we first met?"

She nodded.

"Do you remember when I said that I'd like to be friends?"

Her puzzlement was reflected in the expression on her face. "Yes."

"I want more than that. I guess I've been lying to myself, as well, pretending that you were a friend, someone to spend time with, someone to tease, to have as a companion." He cupped her face in his hands. "But the thing is . . ." He stared at the light that seemed to glow from within her. "I want everything with you. I know it's too soon. We haven't known each other that long, but think about it for the next few days. I want you in my future." He leaned down and pressed his lips softly against hers. With his lips still brushing across hers, he said, "Don't ever leave me. I'm not sure I could survive a life without you somewhere in it."

His kiss confirmed what he was saying . . . and more. His kiss expressed what he could find no words to say. He was trembling, but he didn't care. Never had he felt so vulnerable, as though his heart was in her hands, waiting to see what she would do with it.

Melissa wrapped her arms around his waist, holding him tightly, and returned his kiss. He could feel her heart racing . . . or was that his? Her quickened breathing was no less rushed than his.

Joel discovered that it wasn't always necessary to hear the words in order to understand the meaning. Melissa had answered him. God help them both.

When Melissa finally opened her eyes the next morning, the sun was once again high in the sky. She sighed and slowly stretched, remembering the night before.

Whatever else he was, Joel Kramer was a gentleman. He had known by her response to him last night how she felt about him, but he had not used the knowledge to take advantage of her.

Was she a little disappointed? she wondered with a slight smile on her face. Perhaps, just a little. She found life more confusing than ever before. Living with her head in a book had been much simpler. Somewhere in the printed page, she had always been able to find an answer. Now she didn't know where to look to find an answer to what she felt whenever Joel was nearby. He didn't make her confusion any easier.

She enjoyed him, but she didn't always understand him. There were times when he became introspective, as though he'd withdrawn from her. Perhaps all writers were like that. Maybe he was getting ideas for his novel.

What she needed to do was to relax and enjoy his company without any expectations for the outcome of the relationship. He'd admitted that he was attracted to her. That was a start. After all, they hadn't known each other but a few weeks. Sometimes it was hard for her to remember that.

Now was the time to allow herself to relax and enjoy their growing relationship. What better surroundings could she have chosen than this beautiful tropical paradise?

She rubbed her head where a steady ache seemed to be focused, no doubt caused by the consumption of those powerful drinks they'd sampled last night. Perhaps she wouldn't enjoy herself quite *that* much again.

"Good morning."

Joel stood in the doorway of her room, holding two cups of coffee.

Melissa leaned up on one elbow and pushed her hair from her face. "Good morning. It looks as though I overslept again."

He grinned and advanced into the room. Handing her one of the cups, he said, "Isn't that what vacations are for? No schedules, no appointments." The look in his eyes as he gazed at her made her feel warm. "Besides I haven't been up that long, myself. I don't know about you, but my head felt close to exploding this morning. That rum punch last night was more potent than I gave it credit for."

He sounded relaxed and comfortable being in her bedroom. Melissa fought the impulse to grab the sheet and pull it under her chin. She certainly didn't need to act like somebody's maiden aunt. Not with Joel. Instead, she took a sip from the proffered cup and smiled her pleasure at the delicious taste.

"Did you sleep well?" she asked. She noticed that he didn't meet her eyes before answering.

"Well enough. What would you like to do today?"

She glanced out the window. "Swim and lie out in the sun. We didn't get a chance yesterday, with all our shopping."

He grinned. "I think that can be arranged." He nodded toward the kitchen. "Our driver last night recommended a woman who lives nearby who would be willing to prepare meals for us. I talked with her this morning, and she agreed. She's in the kitchen now, planning some island dishes for us.''

''I think coffee is about all I can handle at this moment. Maybe after my shower, I'll be able to face something a little more substantial.''

Joel turned and started out of the room, then paused. ''I hope you'll thank your friend for me for allowing us to come down here. It's nice to get away from the phone and television and our regular routine.''

She smiled. ''Thank you for successfully promoting the idea of a vacation. Already, I feel like a new person.'' Being with Joel had already done that, but she didn't want to tell him that. She'd confessed too much last night. ''You managed to make relaxing seem like a skilled art. Maybe that's part of being a writer.''

''I suppose.''

Joel left before he could say anything more. He'd be glad when he could tell her what he really did. Would it make a difference to her? She had her own career. Would it bother her that he traveled for weeks at a time? Would she be willing to spend time with him whenever he returned home? How could he ask her until he was free to tell her everything?

He'd called Max last night from a pay phone and explained that there was no phone in the cottage. Max had said things were heating up but hadn't gone into any details. It was only a matter of a couple of days and Joel would be able to tell her the truth.

In the meantime, he was going to forget everything but the moment. He'd been given the gift of time and the opportunity to share that time with Melissa. Because their future was too important to take chances with, he was determined not to pursue closer intimacy with her.

He found her innocence endearing, but once he realized how little she had experienced, he made up his mind not to take advantage of their present situation. If the explosion hadn't occurred when it did, would she have given herself to him? Would he have had the strength to refuse such a gift?

He didn't want to be tested again.

In no way did he ever want her to feel that he had taken advantage of her. So he would wait, even if he had to spend more sleepless nights tossing and turning, knowing that she was just in the next room, knowing that she probably wouldn't refuse him.

With fresh resolve, Joel returned to the kitchen and the woman who was preparing various dishes for them to eat at their convenience. She smiled at him.

"Your wife is up now?"

How to answer that one. "Uh, she isn't hungry just now. We'll probably eat later."

The woman smiled and said nothing. What was there in that knowing smile that made him think she was picturing a well-loved wife who was slow to leave the bed shared with her husband the previous night? Joel almost groaned aloud at the thought.

He gazed out at the water, hoping it was cold enough to take care of what he was afraid was going to be a permanent condition.

Melissa stepped off the porch onto the path that led to the beach. She clutched the beach jacket that she had pulled on to cover the sparse swimsuit she had bought the day before. Whatever had possessed her to think she could wear it anywhere outside of the tiny dressing room in which she had first tried it on? She remembered thinking that the suit would help the new image she hoped to create. However, stripping down to two tiny pieces of material just now had unnerved her more than she thought possible.

She had told Joel to go ahead, that she would be out later. Now she lifted her hand to shade her eyes, looking for him. There he was, swimming out toward the reef that protected the cove from heavier waves. Melissa realized she felt a sense of reprieve that he would not see her as soon as she arrived.

She knew that she would have to get over this ridiculous shyness about being around him. He treated her with patience, understanding and a warmth that made her heart start pounding as soon as he came into view.

The problem was she had never had a relationship with a man before; at least, nothing like this. He seemed to find it natural and normal to spend the day together, kiss her senseless each evening, then bid her a casual goodnight at her bedroom door. It had taken her hours to get to sleep the night before. She felt as though all of her motors were running at top speed. She didn't have a clue how to turn them down or shut them off. Somehow, she'd discovered, her switches were controlled by Joel's presence.

With a determined lift of her chin Melissa followed the path to the beach and with a sense of bravado, removed the jacket and tossed it down beside her towel on the sand. She marched toward the water.

She knew she didn't have Joel's experience in hiding his reactions to her. She also knew that he found her attractive. Therefore, she had no reason to cower behind her fears of allowing him to see her so scantily clad. She could deal with it. After all, she was in the midst of an exciting adventure, and she intended to make the most of their time together.

The waves curled around her feet and she smiled. The water felt wonderful—silky and enticing. A sudden sense of euphoria swept over her and she took several running steps and leapt into the next lazy wave approaching the shore.

When she came up for air, she was breathless and laughing. Why hadn't she discovered earlier how much life had to offer outside of the laboratory? She'd had no idea that she could enjoy the feel of the water and sun stroking her body, could savor the scent of the tropical foliage and flowers, could find the delectable taste of the native fruit so pleasurable.

Melissa swam out into the lagoon until the water rippled gently. Then she rolled onto her back and floated, her eyes closed.

She lost track of time, enjoying the soft caress of the warm sunlight on her face. She'd rubbed a sun block that was supposed to be waterproof all over her body before coming outside. She lazily reminded herself to add more once she got out of the water, but for now, she remained content to enjoy the moment.

Something tugged at her heels and she gasped, luckily filling her lungs with air before she went under the water. Panicked, she floundered until strong arms wrapped around her and pulled her to the surface. She and Joel broke through the surface of the water, their faces only a few inches apart.

"You scared me!" she accused, gasping for air.

"I realized that too late to do much about it. I thought you heard me swimming up to you."

Melissa became aware of their respective positions. She had a death grip around his neck. His arms held her tightly against him so that she could feel his lithe, mostly unclothed body pressed firmly against hers. He felt cool to the touch, which surprised her. She felt scalded everywhere her bare flesh touched his.

She loosened her grip around his neck, and he obligingly allowed his hands to slide down her back and fasten at her waist.

"You okay now?" he asked, and she saw the concern in his eyes.

She smiled. "I must have been more than half asleep. Sorry I overreacted."

He continued to hold her, and she became aware of the fact that their legs were intertwined. Her thigh was tucked intimately between his. She jerked away from him.

"What's wrong?"

"Nothing."

"Are you ready to go back?"

She nodded, avoiding his eyes. He swam beside her when she headed for shore. She briefly closed her eyes, wishing she didn't have such a strong reaction to the man. He gave no indication that he even noticed that she was a member of the opposite sex.

By the time they reached the spot where she'd left her towel, Melissa had managed to gain some control over her behavior. Joel picked up a blanket from nearby that he must have brought down earlier and spread it in the shade. As soon as he sat down, he patted the space beside him.

Melissa kneeled down. He stretched out and closed his eyes. "This is a life I could get used to," he murmured with a smile.

She glanced around, wondering if it would be too obvious if she were to put her jacket back on, then decided it would be. After all, she wanted a tan, didn't she? She searched through her bag for her lotion and applied it vigorously to her arms and legs.

"Need some help?"

Startled, she glanced around. Joel was watching her from beneath lowered eyelids. "I can do it."

"You missed some large areas on your back. Lie down and I'll finish for you."

She closed her eyes and handed him the bottle. With careful strokes, he covered her back, then handed the lotion back to her. He hadn't lingered or given her the impression that he was doing more than helping a friend.

After recapping the bottle, she lay down beside him. "Do you have enough room?" he asked lazily.

"Ummhmm."

"Melissa?"

Her eyes flew open of their own accord. There was a change in his tone of voice.

"Yes?"

"Tell me about your childhood."

She relaxed slightly. "What about it?"

"What did you do for fun?"

She closed her eyes once again and thought back to her early days. "Actually, I don't recall having a childhood."

"What do you mean?"

"I think I was a surprise to my parents. I don't think they ever really wanted a family, but, of course, accepted the fact they were going to be parents with their usual attitude of doing whatever was necessary."

"Is that why you were an only child?"

"Oh, yes. They obviously learned from their mistakes."

"And they considered you to be a mistake?"

She thought about that for a moment. "I really don't know. I never heard them say anything like that, exactly. But there was an attitude that I felt all the time I was growing up. A sense of leashed impatience if I didn't respond immediately to any request they made."

"Is that what you meant about not having a childhood? Didn't you ever get a chance to play?"

"I don't remember much of it, if I did. I started reading at an early age and was soon absorbed in the worlds I could find in books. I started to school quite young. I did well in school. It was the one thing I knew I could do that won my parents' approval. I don't suppose I ever thought about playing."

"Did they ever take you to the seashore when you were small?"

"On occasion, but I was never allowed to play in the water or sand." She smiled. "It was too messy, you understand. I learned very quickly that neat was in, messy was definitely out."

"You once mentioned not having friends. Didn't you miss having someone to share things with?"

"Being known as a brain wasn't conducive to making friends, I'm afraid. Nobody seemed to be interested in anything I had to say."

"Except your parents, maybe?"

She smiled. "Of course. We had nightly discourses around the dinner table, discussing what I had read or learned that day."

"How stimulating for you," he drawled.

Melissa laughed. "You have to understand that I really didn't mind it, since this was the only life I knew. Children are resilient and very adaptable. I felt lucky that I had parents who encouraged me and my curiosity."

"But they didn't teach you to play."

"Well, no, that wasn't part of the curriculum."

Several moments went by before Joel asked, "Didn't you say you met Karen in college?"

Melissa smiled again. "Yes. She was my first and closest friend, even though she was older. She probably taught me everything I know about dating men."

Joel rolled over onto his side and propped himself on his elbow. "Oh, really?"

She opened her eyes and saw him only a few inches away. His eyes were dancing, and she smiled at his expression.

"Tell me more," he invited in a soft voice.

She shrugged. "Karen used to come back to the dorm after a date and tell me what had happened—the places they went, some of the moves the guys tried. You know."

He widened his eyes slightly. "I haven't the foggiest. I never finished college."

She swatted at him. "You know what I mean. The kinds of things that all guys try."

He placed his hand on her bare waist. "Ohhh, I understand. You mean moves, like this."

Melissa felt her stomach muscles quiver. "I don't think she charted each and every one, but I wouldn't be surprised if that was one of them."

"And did she tell you what to do in case a man carried on in such a reprehensible manner?"

"You're making fun of me."

"A little," he agreed.

"Why?"

"I suppose because I find you such a contradictory person to be around. You're highly intelligent, no doubt very knowledgeable in your field, but every time I get within a few feet of you, you tense up as though you're expecting me to attack you. Is it me that makes you nervous, or all men?''

''You don't make me nervous,'' she said in a softly defiant tone.

He moved his hand so that he cupped her breast. She inhaled sharply. ''I don't? Then why is your heart beating so fast?''

She closed her eyes, trying to think. She had to be nonchalant in order to let him know that she was willing to pursue their relationship in whatever form it took. ''You startled me, that's all.''

''I'm not surprised. There's no telling what nefarious schemes I might be pursuing now that I have you here alone.''

''I sincerely doubt that any scheme you might be dreaming up is either wicked or villainous.''

He leaned closer, so that his mouth was only an inch or so away from hers. ''But you aren't absolutely certain, are you?''

She blinked. ''Not absolutely, no.''

''So you're aware I could take advantage of your trusting nature, aren't you?''

Before she could find an answer, he took the opportunity to respond away from her. His mouth covered hers in a persuasive kiss that caused all of her thinking processes to shut down. She touched his shoulder with her fingertips. The satiny smoothness of his skin coaxed her to explore. She traced the hard muscles bunched there and was intrigued by the contrast of skin and sinew.

Melissa felt as though her heart was going to pound its way right out of her chest. This man had such a strong effect on her that her response to him frightened her. It was that realization that caused her to turn her face away from him.

She could feel his fingers resting lightly against her breast. Their heat seared through the material as though each finger would be permanently imprinted there.

He touched her cheeks and gently turned her head until she was looking at him once more. "You can trust me, Melissa. I want you to know that."

She felt herself slipping into the magic of his gaze.

"I suppose you're used to this sort of thing." She waved her hand toward the surroundings. "I just feel a little out of my depth here."

He closed his eyes for a moment. "Believe me," he said after a moment, "so do I."

"You mean this is unusual for you, too?"

"Very."

She smiled. "I'm glad. You seem to be adjusting to everything that's happened more readily than I am. I've envied your ability to adapt."

Joel felt anything but relaxed at the moment.

She went on. "You're the first man that I've ever spent so much time with on a social basis. I always felt so awkward, never knowing what to say. But with you, it's been different."

"In what way?"

She shrugged. "Oh, I don't know. I guess you've allowed me to be me without feeling self-conscious about my lack of social skills."

"Melissa. There is absolutely nothing lacking in your social skills. You need to let go of that image of yourself. You're warm...and friendly...and very cuddly...and—" He leaned down and kissed her once again. "And I'll always be thankful I found you."

Her gaze returned to him. "You will?"

He nodded.

She touched his cheek. "I feel the same way."

They lay there together on the blanket and looked at each other in silence. Joel knew that he'd never needed his iron control more than he did then. He could see the shy yearning in her eyes and knew that she would not stop him from making love to her. She had no idea how tempted he was to do just that.

Before Melissa could give her actions too much thought, she slid her hand behind his head and pulled him down to her until their lips met. This time, she would not fight the feelings. This time, she was willing to explore the unknown.

# *Chapter Eight*

"Is she getting restless to return home?" Max asked.

"She hasn't said. I've kept her busy—taught her how to snorkel, rented a small sailboat as well as a car to explore the island."

Melissa had gone to buy souvenirs for some of the people in her office, and Joel had taken the opportunity to call Max from a pay phone nearby.

"Has she said anything about needing to get back to work?"

"She called and talked to one of the management heads who told her there were still problems to be worked out before the building could be reopened. She plans to call again tomorrow."

"Then it sounds to me as though everything is under control."

"How's Feldman?"

"He's doing well. Working full-time and seems to be excited about his latest experiment."

"Has he asked about Melissa?"

"Only to be certain she was all right. The bombing really upset him."

"It managed to put a few wrinkles in my plans, as well."

"Are you trying to tell me you would prefer to be up here dealing with the ice and sleet? If so, I'm sure we can figure a way to bring her back and put her under surveillance."

"Did I say that? I'm just a little concerned over how long this whole matter is taking. The last time we talked, you said this thing should be over in a couple of days. That was almost a week ago."

"I know that's what I said. But there's no timetable on situations like this. We're doing everything we can."

"One of the local restaurants agreed to take my calls and said they'd get word to me. Let me know the minute this thing is taken care of, will you?"

"You know, Kramer, I'm really getting worried about you. There you are on a tropical island with a beautiful woman, and all you can talk about is finishing the job."

What Joel wanted was the release of the need to stay with his cover. As soon as the matter was dealt with, he intended to explain everything to Melissa.

Then he intended to ask her to marry him.

However, he had no intention of explaining any of this to Max.

"You know how dedicated I am to my work," he drawled, causing Max to laugh.

"The inactivity getting to you?"

"Let's just say I'm ready to forget about my career as a writer."

"Just remember to keep Dr. Jordan happy, okay?"

"I'm doing my very best, boss. Talk to you later."

Joel hung up and turned away from the phone. His frustration level continued to escalate the longer the time they spent together. He didn't want to do anything to betray the growing trust she had in him. He felt as though he held a very delicate flower in his hands that he could easily crush and destroy if he were to mishandle it.

Melissa had taught him so much about himself and his own attitudes of distrust toward people. She believed in the basic goodness of everyone. He had reason to know that a person could get killed believing in people. And yet he didn't want to awaken her to the darker aspects of life. He wanted to continue to protect her from so much.

"Joel?"

He turned around to find Melissa standing there, holding a large bag.

"I take it you decided to buy one of everything in the shop."

She laughed. "Just about. Thank you for loaning me the money."

"No problem."

She glanced at her watch. "If we're going to do any snorkeling today, we'd better get back."

"My thoughts exactly."

They smiled at each other. He caught her hand and led her to the car.

During the drive to the cottage, Melissa asked, "Are you getting restless about not writing?"

"Why do you ask?"

"I heard you pacing in your room last night. Then later, I saw you walking along the beach."

Joel glanced at Melissa, trying to read the expression on her face. "You should have joined me."

"I assumed you wanted to be alone."

Joel wasn't sure how to respond. Most of his nights were restless with very short periods of sleep. Being around Melissa all day, every day, was definitely having its effect on him.

When he didn't respond, she asked, "Why don't we go home?"

Joel slowed and turned into the driveway. As he parked the car, he asked, "Is that what you want?"

"I think that's what *you* want."

His grin was meant to reassure her. "Given the choice of swimming in the Caribbean or sweating over a manuscript in the frozen north, I much prefer the water." He got out of the car and walked around to open her door. "But if you're getting bored—"

"It isn't that."

Melissa wasn't sure what it was that was bothering her, but she knew that Joel wasn't being completely honest with her. He was too restless to be enjoying himself as much as he wanted her to believe.

In the days since they had arrived, he had kept them on such a busy schedule that she fell into bed each night exhausted. She almost longed for the sedate days of the laboratory, even though she had to admit she looked and felt better than she had for some time.

Her skin had turned the color of toast; her hair had lightened considerably, with streaks of platinum mixed in with the darker blond, and the regimen of daily swimming had toned up her muscles considerably.

Considering all their activities, she found it surprising that Joel had the energy for midnight walks . . . and the other morning she had spotted him on the beach doing push ups! Like everything else, he'd laughed off her questions.

But she could read the signs; he was becoming bored with her.

Unfortunately, the same wasn't true for her. The more she was around him, the more she wanted to be around him. Even worse, she finally recognized the malady that explained all of her symptoms lately. She was in love with Joel Kramer.

He'd admitted that he wanted to be more than friends, but had made no moves to deepen their intimacy. She still cringed when she thought back to the night when she'd offered herself to him. He must have thought her totally brazen. He was probably relieved that he hadn't had to respond, even though she distinctly remembered him heading toward the bedroom with her.

But he hadn't mentioned that scene since. She had wondered if he would once they were alone on the island. He continued to kiss her until she became limp; he continued to caress her until her body came vibratingly alive; and he continued to sleep alone.

Melissa hadn't a clue what all of that meant, other than the obvious: he was driving her out of her mind.

"I'll meet you on the beach in fifteen minutes," he said as soon as they walked inside the house.

Melissa wandered back into the bedroom and put away the items she'd bought that morning. She slipped into her bikini, no longer self-conscious about wearing it around him.

He was waiting for her by the water's edge when she arrived, their gear lying at his feet. Melissa was glad she wore her sunglasses to shield her eyes. She would have been embarrassed if he knew how much she enjoyed looking at him in his bathing trunks. His dark tan had deepened, and his brown hair had lightened in streaks, much like hers. She had to stop herself from reaching out to touch his muscled chest, from smoothing her hand across that broad expanse, from tracing the way the hair grew into a path that led downward across his stomach and abdomen.

She jerked her gaze upward to meet his.

"Ready?"

She nodded, unable to trust her voice at the moment.

Joel knelt and slipped the flippers onto her feet, then handed her the mouthpiece and goggles. "There you go." She gave him a cheerful wave and waded into the water.

Later, Joel realized that he should have known disaster would hit before the day was over. Things kept happening...unusual and unpredictable things. The strap on his mask broke, Melissa kept having trouble with one of her flippers, and he scraped his hand on some coral.

They spent the afternoon exploring the reef and all its myriad inhabitants. He trusted Melissa in the water now, even though he continued to keep a close eye on her. When he saw the snake slide out from between the coral, he tried to warn her, but he was too late. Nor was he close enough to prevent the snake from striking Melissa as she swam too close to its territory. By the time Joel reached her side, she had doubled over and sunk below the surface.

He'd seen the snake's distinctive markings and knew that it was poisonous. Within a few short minutes, the venom would get into her bloodstream and no one would be able to help her.

The time spent in the Central America jungles had trained him well and he knew what he had to do. Pulling her, he swam toward the shore as soon as he got her head out of the water. When he reached land, he stripped off his footgear and, with Melissa held securely in his arms, broke into a run.

Joel jerked the mask off her face to make sure she could breathe. Her face looked white beneath her tan. He was thankful that she had fainted.

He got her inside the house and placed her on her bed, then sprinted to the kitchen where he found a knife. Taking precious seconds to sterilize the blade, he rushed back to where she lay. From what he could see, the snake had struck her on the hip. He jerked down the minuscule bikini bottoms and saw the angry red marks on her upper thigh, near the groin area. Once again, he blessed her unconsciousness as he sliced an $X$ over the wound and began to draw out the poison with his mouth.

Joel worked on her for several minutes, praying that he hadn't lost too much time getting her to the house. When at last he paused, she was shaking from shock and chills.

He made a poultice to place over the wound, then wrapped her in a sheet and covered her with blankets. He lost track of time while he sat beside her, holding her hand and praying.

Eventually, she stirred and opened her eyes. She seemed to be having trouble focusing. She blinked a couple of times, then whispered, "Joel?"

He tightened the hold he had on her hand. She had been growing increasingly warmer and now felt hot to the touch. "I'm right here. Just relax and try to rest."

"What happened?"

"You got a poisonous bite."

She closed her eyes. "I don't remember anything. I just remember being in the water, then feeling this horrible pain, and…" She shifted restlessly, then opened her eyes and focused on him. "I feel so strange," she whispered.

"You're going to be okay," he said, praying that he spoke the truth. "The poultice is drawing out the poison

I didn't get out. But you're going to feel the effects, I'm afraid.''

She was having trouble swallowing. After a moment, she whispered, ''I'm glad you knew what to do.''

*I hope to hell it works,* he thought. He wiped the moisture that had collected on his brow. ''Try to rest, okay?''

''I could have drowned.''

''No. That would never have happened. You know I wouldn't allow anything to happen to you.''

She was so pale. Her lips were almost white when she smiled and said, ''You're always saving me.''

''Doesn't matter.''

She drifted off to sleep.

The next several hours were hell for Joel as he watched her fight the effects of the snake bite. She alternated between chills and fever, fighting the covers and resisting his efforts to keep liquids going down her.

At one point, he stretched out beside her and held her against him until she quietened.

He must have dozed, because it was the sound of her voice that awakened him later. He glanced at his watch. It was after two in the morning.

Once again, she fought the covers, muttering incoherently.

''But don't you understand?'' she asked in a querulous voice. ''I love him and I don't know what to do,'' she complained.

Joel had been reaching for the cloth that he'd been using to bathe her face when he caught her words. They slammed into his chest like a fist, taking his breath. She was in love with someone? Why hadn't she ever mentioned him? They had spent so many hours sharing their lives with each other. He'd felt as though he knew everything of any importance about her. But she had been hiding something from him. A knot of pain formed in his throat.

He placed the wet cloth gently against her forehead and wiped away the dampness there, stricken.

"I don't know what to do," she whimpered. "He holds me and kisses me, but then walks away. And he seems so restless..." Her voice faded into mutterings before she said quite clearly, "Maybe he only wants to be my friend! I don't want to lose him because I wanted more."

Joel realized that she was talking about him and released the air he'd been unconsciously holding. She loved him. There was no one else. He felt relief flooding through him like a drug, easing his anxiety, relaxing the muscles he'd tensed when she'd started muttering.

He continued to bathe her body in an effort to bring down the fever. She could not seem to lie still. Her limbs kept jerking, and she kept tossing her head. He discovered that she quieted down whenever he talked to her. For hours, he kept a soft litany of words flowing until he was hoarse, but it worked. She appeared more calm and allowed him to stroke her body with the cooling cloth.

She was so beautiful. Her skin felt like satin, and he found himself touching her to reassure himself that she would be all right. She just had to be. He broke out in a cold sweat thinking about what had happened. The snake had struck without warning. He could have lost her in that same quick way.

The early-morning hours seemed filled with his quiet contemplation. Now that he knew how she felt about him, he could no longer accept his decision to wait before claiming her. The job could go on for weeks more.

He loved her and he wanted her. She knew him better than anyone did, including Max. What difference did it make, after all, how he made a living? He pictured them together when he told her the truth. In his vision, she laughed at his fears and reassured him of her love.

So why wait for the nebulous end of this assignment? There really wasn't a problem, was there, once she was well again. Surely God wouldn't allow her to appear in his life only to take her away.

Joel never wanted to experience the fear of losing her again. He'd faced death himself. In fact, he'd been more dead than alive when they'd brought him back from Central America last year. The fear of dying hadn't affected him as strongly as the fear of losing Melissa.

Pale fingers of light entered the room and Joel looked around. Dawn was approaching. He leaned over and turned off the small lamp beside Melissa's bed. In the dim shadows of the room, she lay there, breathing evenly, and he realized that her fever had broken.

Thank God! Tears came to his eyes and he blinked fiercely to prevent them from falling. She was going to be all right.

He eased away from her and went into the other room for fresh sheets. He carefully changed the damp bed linens while she remained in a deep, healing slumber.

Then he walked into his room and sat on the edge of the bed to take off his shoes. Later he never remembered falling across the bed in a sound sleep.

Melissa felt as though she'd been hit over the head repeatedly with a sledgehammer. She groaned, unable to deal quietly with the pulsating ache.

"Here's something for the pain. It should help."

She opened her eyes at the sound of Joel's deep voice. Bright sunlight found its way through the chinked slats at the window, and she winced, closing her eyes. She felt his arm slide beneath her shoulders, raising her slightly.

"Open your mouth," he said, not bothering to hide his amusement at the tone he'd used, as though speaking to a child. She obliged him and he placed a tablet on her tongue, then held a glass to her lips.

The liquid was refreshing to her parched mouth and she took several swallows.

"Thank you," she murmured.

He returned her to the pillow, sliding a second one beneath her. "Do you think you could eat something?"

"I think so." Once again, she opened her eyes, forcing herself to adjust to the long slivers of light. "I'm sorry to be so much trouble."

She'd never seen him look like this. Dark smudges beneath his eyes made him look as though he hadn't slept in several days. Stubble framed his lower face, and his eyes were swollen and rimmed with red. He rubbed his hand across his jaw and made a face. "I'm just glad to see you awake and coherent. I don't mind admitting that you had me worried for a while last night."

She didn't understand why she felt so weak. She started to move and her head began an increased pounding.

Melissa touched her head, rubbing her fingertips across her brow.

"That tablet should help with the pain in a few minutes." He moved away from the bed toward the door.

"Joel?"

He glanced around at her, his eyes wary. "Yes?"

"Thank you."

His smile flashed in his dark face, causing her heart to do crazy things in her chest. "Any time."

It was only after he left the room that Melissa realized she was nude. When had he removed her swim suit? She lifted the sheet and gazed at the poultice placed over the wound. Her face flamed at its location. She certainly didn't have any secrets from the man now!

Despite the pounding in her head, she knew she had to get up. She had to go to the bathroom, and she certainly wasn't going to have him help her! Taking her time, Melissa slid her legs off the bed, then carefully stood up. Her legs felt like overcooked spaghetti. Only through sheer determination did she manage, by holding on to various pieces of furniture, to get to the bathroom. Afterward, she splashed water on her face and looked into the mirror.

Sunken eyes with deep circles around them stared back at her, and her hair tumbled around her shoulders in a mat of tangles. Really glamorous, she decided ruefully.

She managed to return to the bedroom and find a nightgown. She wasn't going anywhere today but bed, and she knew it. As soon as the soft material slid over her body, she felt better, more protected. She was only a few steps from the bed when Joel found her.

"What the hell are you doing!"

He startled her so that she let go of the chair she'd been leaning on. If he hadn't caught her, she would have fallen.

"I had to go to the bathroom," she muttered as soon as he placed her on the bed once more.

"Why didn't you call me?" he demanded.

"I didn't want to bother you."

He shook his head, then turned and picked up the bowl of hot cereal he'd brought into the room with him. He handed it to her. "It's a wonder I didn't spill this when I saw you."

He turned around and walked out of the room without another word, leaving Melissa to feel churlish because she had displeased him when he'd done so much for her.

By the time she finished eating, she could no longer keep her eyes open. She didn't remember Joel coming in later to check on her.

He stood beside the bed, noting that she had found a gown to put on. He'd been so shocked to find her out of bed that he hadn't paid attention at the time to the fact she had managed to dress. He smiled, wishing he could have seen her reaction when she discovered that he had obviously undressed her. It would be interesting to see if she brought up that fact at a later time.

He was pleased to note some color in her cheeks. God, but she'd given him a scare. He never wanted to go through anything like that again.

They were going to have to talk, there was no doubt about that. Considering the way he felt about her, he couldn't let her walk out of his life. All he had to do was convince her that they shouldn't waste this time together.

He couldn't remember when he'd been so nervous. He realized he'd been gruff with her, but he was scared. Scared she wouldn't agree to getting married right away, scared that he would say something to cause her to leave him. Loving someone could be hell, he discovered. Why had he always heard that love was supposed to be wonderful?

If she agreed to marry him, then he could begin to believe the publicity. Right now, he was afraid to believe in much of anything.

They had to talk, but not until she was much better. He didn't want to pressure her. He didn't want to feel as though he had taken advantage of the situation. But the waiting was hard for him. Not knowing could gnaw at a man's guts.

He wouldn't allow himself to think about it. He'd look after her, wait until he felt she was ready to hear what he had to say. In the meantime, he'd continue with the hard physical exercise, the cold showers and the nighttime memories of her beautiful body wearing only the soft lamplight.

## Chapter Nine

Three days passed before Melissa felt well enough to go outside. She sat on the blanket near the water's edge and watched Joel swim toward her.

He'd been wonderful to her these past few days, making sure she was comfortable, looking after her in unobtrusive ways. It certainly wasn't his fault that she'd fallen in love with him. He'd offered her friendship, and like a silly fool, she'd lost her heart.

He came to his feet in the shallows and strode toward her. Would she ever get tired of watching him? she wondered with a pang. He moved with such ease. When he caught her eye, he grinned, the white flash of teeth a deep contrast to his darkly tanned body.

"You're looking like yourself once again," he commented, dropping down beside her on the blanket and grabbing a towel.

"Too bad. I could have auditioned for Methuselah's mother a few days ago with no competition."

He chuckled. "No one looks their best after going through what you just experienced." He tugged her braid. "How long did it take to get the tangles out?"

"Who knows? I seriously considered cutting it off, but I couldn't find anything sharp enough."

"Thank God!" he said. "Your hair is too beautiful to cut."

She shook her head. "This style is hopelessly out of fashion."

"Do you care?"

"It's a little late to care, wouldn't you say? I've never taken the time to follow fashion."

"You know, Melissa, I've been thinking..."

Melissa looked at him in surprise. His tone of voice had changed and his face had sobered from the earlier teasing look. "About what?"

He still held her braid in his hand, and now he studied it with deep regard. "How this island would make a really great place for a honeymoon," he said without glancing up.

She didn't know what to say. Melissa just looked at him, hoping he would explain his remark.

When his gaze finally met hers, her heart suddenly lurched in her chest. She'd never seen that look in his eyes before.

"What are you saying?" she managed to whisper.

"That I want to marry you." The words hung in the air between them, taking on a life of their own.

Melissa continued to stare at him, still not certain that she had heard him correctly. Perhaps she was still in delirium, fighting the ghosts and gremlins produced by her feverish state.

"Did you say...*marry* me?"

He looked away and picked up a handful of sand. Letting it trail through his fingers, he gazed out at the water. "Yeah," he finally muttered hoarsely.

For a moment, she was reminded of the man she'd met all those weeks ago. Dark color filled his cheeks, and she realized once again that Joel could be shy. Not that she'd seen that part of him in some time. He certainly didn't kiss her like a man who was shy. And the way he held and caressed her had certainly shown no tendencies toward shyness.

Now he refused to meet her eyes.

Melissa realized that she had gone into shock at his words. She couldn't feel anything except a tingling numbness. Even in her most creative fantasies, it had never occurred to her that he might love her or want to marry her. She reminded herself that he hadn't said anything about love, but why else would a man propose marriage?

Seen in this suddenly new light, his behavior recently could be perceived in a much different way. He'd been restless, and she had thought he was bored. She'd been restless, as well, but boredom had been the farthest thing from her mind. Frustration had center stage most of the time. Was that his problem?

If so, then he'd been too honorable to take advantage of their present situation. Had they stayed in their own apartments, he would probably have pursued a leisurely affair with her. Because of her strong attraction to him, she would have been more than willing.

But Joel wanted more. Much more.

Was she going to back away from him now that he was offering her the opportunity to spend the rest of her life with the man who had stolen her heart? Of course not!

Then why was she trembling so? Why was she so afraid to speak up, to answer him?

Perhaps cowardice was inherited—a genetic flaw.

"Do you mean that we should get married while we're here on the island?"

He picked up more sand and studied it as though he was certain to find treasure there if he searched vigilantly enough.

"I guess it was a really stupid idea. When you decide to marry, you'll want all your friends there, a big wedding, everything—"

"Joel?" She could only see him in profile. "Would you mind looking at me?" With obvious reluctance, he turned his head. She saw the vulnerability in his eyes and felt herself melting with tenderness and love for this wonderfully strong, yet gentle man. "I can't think of anything more wonderful than to marry you... now... while we're here on the island. My friends would understand. Would yours?"

His relief that she agreed to marry him made him weak, and it took him a moment to realize what she'd asked him.

"My friends?" He thought of Max, who would definitely not understand. "It doesn't matter what my friends think." He took her hand. It looked so delicate lying in his. "Are you sure? I don't want to rush you." Which was a lie. That was exactly what he wanted—to rush her into marriage, to rush her into his bed...and to keep her forever in his arms.

Her smiled sparkled like a thousand-watt light. "I think we both must be crazy to even consider doing something so rash." She thought about the life she'd had before Joel moved into the apartment across from hers. How could she have had any idea that she would have changed so drastically in such a short time. From being a shy introvert, she had discovered a whole new world.

From the day she had first seen him, she had made choices totally unlike her usual behavior. She had to trust herself. She had to trust her own instincts.

"Yes."

He stared at her uncertainly. "Yes?"

She nodded.

"You'll marry me?"

She nodded.

"Now?"

She glanced down at their clothing and smiled. "Perhaps we should try for a bit more formality than this, though. What do you think?"

But Joel was no longer thinking. He grabbed her and held her to him, his mouth searching blindly for hers.

She'd agreed, she was willing to marry him, she was going to be his, she—

He broke away from her and stared down at her dazed expression.

"Dear God, but I love you!" He hauled her back into his arms. "Thank you for trusting me. Thank you for believing in me. You won't regret it. I promise. I would never hurt you. Never. I will always take care of you and protect you. Don't ever forget that I love you."

His kiss reaffirmed his words. Melissa felt lighter than air, as though she were floating. Joel loved her. He wanted to marry her. They could deal with the details of their life together later. After all, they had all the time in the world.

When he finally pulled away from her, his gaze was heated. "Let's go find out what we have to do."

It took three days to fill out the forms, pass the necessary tests and be married before a minister. Three very frustrating days. Joel knew better than to go near Melissa. Not even a saint would have that sort of willpower. Those three days were the longest he'd ever spent. The nights were even worse.

But he left her alone. And he waited.

The simple ceremony was held in the chapel of the only church on the island. Joel didn't care where they were married, just as long as it happened. Melissa had told him that she wanted more than a civil ceremony, and he had agreed. He would have agreed to anything.

The sun was close to setting when they returned home. Joel felt very ill at ease now that he'd managed to accomplish his goal. She was his wife now. He was having trouble realizing that his period of self-restraint and self-denial was over.

He hoped.

"Are you hungry?" Melissa asked, peering into the refrigerator. "The woman you hired left several delicious-looking dishes in here."

"Sounds good." He was pleased that he sounded so casual. "I also bought some champagne."

She glanced around at him, her color high. "I've never had champagne."

"There's always a first time."

Neither one wanted to point out the first times that would occur on their wedding night.

She smiled. "All right," she said, then busied herself pulling food from the refrigerator and warming it. Joel checked to see if the champagne was chilled. It was.

They ate out on the deck by candlelight. After Melissa's second glass of champagne, she began to relax.

"No one at work is going to believe this," she said, setting her glass down.

"Believe what?"

She waved her hand. "All of this." She included the sea, the beach, the tropical foliage, the house…and him. "How am I supposed to tell them that in a few short weeks, I met a man and married him, that we spent a large part of our time together on an island." She shook her head. "Dr. Feldman will think I've finally gone over the edge."

"Dr. Feldman?"

"My boss. I'm sure I've mentioned him to you."

"Possibly."

"He should be back from his vacation by now." She leaned her forearm on the table. "We really need to go back home soon, Joel. I have a job that I must return to."

"I thought you told me the office still had not re-opened."

"Well, I need to at least be there when Dr. Feldman comes back. Surely, he'll do something about getting us back into our lab."

"How do you think he's going to take the idea that you're married?"

"Dr. Feldman? Oh, he won't care. Just as long as I continue to work." She paused as though hit by a sudden thought. "You aren't going to be like some husbands who insist on their wives not working, are you?"

"And if I were?"

"Then you'll have quite a fight on your hands."

He grinned. "Then I'll save my energy for more important things." He almost laughed at the expression on her face. She was so much fun to tease.

They carried the plates and dishes back into the house and quickly washed them. Joel felt that he had waited long enough.

"Melissa?"

"Hmm?" She had her back to him, placing the cleaned plates on the shelf.

"How about another glass of champagne?"

She looked over her shoulder with a grin. "Are you trying to get me drunk?"

"Would it do any good?"

"Do you think you're going to have to coax me to bed?" She turned as she said that and walked over to him.

"Am I?"

She slid her arms around his neck. "I don't think so." Her lips brushed lightly against his, but it was enough to start a blaze from the smoldering emotions that he'd kept forcibly under control. Without another word, he slipped his arms around her, picked her up and headed toward the bedroom. The kiss continued until they both had to pause for air. Then Joel allowed his bride to slide from his arms until she was standing beside the bed.

He forced himself to take his time as he carefully removed each piece of clothing she wore. He'd seen her body before, when she'd been so ill, but now she was vibrantly healthy and he wanted her so much, he ached.

She reached up and began to unbutton his shirt. "You're ahead of me," she managed to say, tugging at his belt. That was the only encouragement he needed to assist her.

The only light in the room came from the moon. There was enough to see each other in the shadows, but not the expressions on each face. Joel sank onto the edge of the bed.

He pulled her so that she was standing between his legs. "I don't want to rush you," he said in a low voice, sliding his hands along her sides. He could feel her body quiver as his fingers trailed across the sides of her breasts, circled around her waist, then caught the top of her panties. He slid them down her legs. When she stepped out of that last article of clothing, he cupped his hands around her curving derriere and pulled her closer, placing a kiss on her navel.

She shivered at his touch.

Tentatively, she placed her hands across his shoulders, then slid them along his neck until she framed his jawline. She sank down on one of his thighs and lightly brushed his lips with hers. "I don't know what's expected of me. I don't want to be a disappointment to you."

He groaned and hugged her to him. "You could never be a disappointment, sweet one, don't you understand that? I've been so afraid I was going to lose you from my life. I wouldn't let myself think about the fact that you'd agree to marry me for fear I would jinx the wedding somehow. I kept expecting someone to burst through the doorway in an attempt to stop us."

She touched his chest. At long last, she could give in to the temptation that had made her fingers itch for weeks. She ran the tips of them through the short curls that matted his chest, luxuriating in the feel of him.

He leaned back slowly until he lay across the bed. "That feels good," he said in a husky voice.

"I'm glad. I've wanted so badly to touch you."

"Then why didn't you?"

"I was afraid you wouldn't like it."

"You must be joking!"

Melissa knew that she was far from stupid. She had a string of degrees to prove differently. She'd studied the human anatomy—the male human anatomy—and was fully cognizant of all the moving parts. So why was she being so shy about seeing the man she loved . . . her husband, for Pete's sake . . . totally without adornment?

A silly reaction, but real, nonetheless.

Lying beside him, she determinedly accepted the gift he was offering—the opportunity to explore and get to know him physically. Ignoring shyness, she placed her hands on his stomach. She was gratified to see that his skin rippled at her touch. With a caress that barely skimmed the surface of his skin, she began her exploration.

She discovered the sensitivity of his flat nipples where they nestled in the silky hair. When she brushed lightly across the tip of one of them, it hardened into a tiny nubbin that fascinated her. She leaned down and gently flicked her tongue across the sensitive point.

His body jerked as though he'd been electrocuted.

"Good God, woman!"

She lifted her head and smiled at him, then continued her discoveries. Now that he was no longer encumbered with clothing, she could follow the course of chest hair as it narrowed down his body. She followed the path with her fingers until she touched him on the most sensitive part of his body.

Once again he jerked.

"I can't stand much more of this!"

"Of what?" she asked innocently.

With a move so sudden she wasn't prepared for it, Joel rolled over, pinning her.

"I'll show you," he muttered, stringing a row of tiny kisses down along her collarbone and continuing down to the peak of her breast. He ignored her squirming and proceeded to leisurely lave the pink tip with his tongue, rolling it in his mouth. She gasped when he pulled on it lightly with his lips, then she hugged him closer.

Melissa forgot her inexperience; she forgot her shyness; she forgot everything about Joel and what he was doing to her. He touched sensitive places on her body that she had never considered before—the bend of her elbow, the back of her knee, her inner thigh. He seemed to know exactly where to caress her. She felt as though her body was a musical instrument being played by a master musician. She knew that if she listened closely enough, she would be able to hear her body hum, like the tautened string of a violin.

By the time he paused, kneeling between her legs, she felt lost in the wonder of what they were sharing. She also felt blessed to be able to experience this ultimate sharing with the man she loved.

"I don't want to hurt you," he whispered, leaning over her, braced by his hands on each side of her face.

"You could never hurt me, Joel. I know that." With complete confidence in him, she drew him down as she lifted her body to meet him.

Because of his patience and her trust, their joining was a small discomfort compared to the pleasure they both received when he claimed her fully as his. He sank deeply into her warmth, knowing that he had come home at last. She was his, and he would never let her go.

Sometime during the night, Joel roused enough to realize that a breeze had sprung up. Melissa curled close to his side. He rubbed his hand across her arm and felt the tiny chills that rippled her skin. Without waking her, he reached down for the covers and carefully tucked the sheet around both of them.

She looked so young, lying there in his arms. There was little more than ten years difference between them in age, but millions of years difference in life-styles and experience. She had given him back so much that he thought was lost from his life: youth, love, vitality, enthusiasm, joy. It would take him the rest of his life to show her his love and appreciation for all that she was.

It was a task he looked forward to accomplishing.

## Chapter Ten

The steady pounding finally impinged on Joel's consciousness, at least to the point where he managed to focus on the fact that he was going to have to do something to stop it. He groaned and rolled over in bed.

After forcing his eyes open, he became aware of two things: one...someone was banging on the front door, and two...he was not alone in bed. Only then did he recall the events of the previous day: he and Melissa were married.

The pounding continued its steady cadence. Whoever it was certainly personified the word *persistent*. "Damn it," he muttered to himself. *Doesn't anyone have any respect for a newly wedded couple?*

But then, few people were aware of their new status. Joel tried to muffle a groan as he rolled into a sitting position, swung his legs to the floor and forced himself onto his feet.

His head hurt. Champagne always gave him a headache. So did lack of sleep. He glanced at the sleeping woman beside him and smiled. The constant pounding hadn't disturbed her. After all, she hadn't gotten any more sleep than he had, and how could he possibly sleep for long stretches of time when, even in his sleep, he was aware of her pressed so intimately against him.

He grabbed his jeans and pulled them on, zipping as he walked toward the door. He jerked the door open to growl at whoever had the audacity to make such an ungodly noise, only to recognize the culprit. It was the teenage son of the owner of the restaurant.

"Sorry to bother you. My dad said there was a call for you and that it was very important. You're to call your office right away."

Joel dug into his pocket and pulled out a folded bill. "Thanks," he said, handing the boy the money.

The boy bobbed his head and ran back to his bicycle.

His office. Max's code to call him. Joel ran his hand through his hair, rumpling it further. Damn. He'd been doing a hell of a job blotting out the rest of the world, Max in particular, ever since Melissa had been injured. He hadn't worried about what was happening back in the States because he no longer cared. He could stay here with Melissa from now on, now that their future had been decided.

Unfortunately, the world had its own way of intruding, no matter how hard he concentrated on forgetting all about it.

He turned around and headed for his bedroom. He needed to get some shoes on, grab a shirt and go find out what Max wanted. Once he was dressed, he peeked into the other bedroom. Melissa hadn't moved. With any luck at all, he'd be back in bed with her before she even knew he'd left.

"Why haven't you called in this week?" were Max's first words. "I have some news."

Joel fumbled for the nearest chair by the pay phone in the small restaurant, drew it closer, and sat down. He knew that tone of voice. He was going to be here for a while.

"I was busy," he said. He signaled a waiter for a cup of coffee, then asked, "What's happened?"

Max ignored his question. "Did it ever occur to you that I might be worried when you didn't contact me on schedule?"

"No," Joel replied truthfully. He knew his boss too well to think that he might possess such human qualities.

"Is Melissa all right?"

Memories of the previous day and evening flitted through Joel's mind. "I think so."

"What do you mean, you *think* so? Don't you know?"

"She's all right, damn it. We just didn't get much sleep last night."

Max absorbed that piece of news in silence for a moment. "Would you like to elaborate on that a little?"

"No, I wouldn't. So, what's your news?"

"We managed to round up the group who were after Feldman and your charge," Max responded without inflection.

"God! There's a relief."

"I thought you'd want to know. Of course, they're denying knowing anything about the wreck or the bombing, but we've got enough evidence on them that it's only going to be a matter of time before they start trying to plea bargain.''

"So we can come home now," Joel said slowly, trying to think through what needed to be done next. Now he could tell Melissa everything. There was no longer a need for secrecy. What a relief that was going to be.

"Yes. As a matter of fact, I have another assignment for you."

"I see."

"It's more in your line than what you've been doing, so I think you'll like it. However, I'm keeping you out of Central America for a while. I need you in Southeast Asia."

"Uh, Max. There's been a new development in this case that I haven't bothered discussing with you."

"What's that?"

"Well..." He stopped to clear his throat. "I, uh... That is, we decided that..." He kneaded the muscles in the back of his neck. "Melissa and I were married yesterday."

"You were *what?*"

Joel flinched and jerked the phone away from his ear. Somehow, he'd known that his boss wouldn't take that particular piece of news well. He could hardly blame Max, under the circumstances.

"Are you out of your mind? That's the most unethical stunt I've ever known you to pull, Kramer."

"Do I sound like I'm bragging?"

"So you've blown your cover and gotten married."

"I didn't say that. Since I'm using my own name, there was no problem providing identification."

"Are you telling me she thinks she married a writer?"

"Yes."

"Oh, God."

Joel ran his hand through his hair, so that it was standing in several spikes. "I don't think it's going to make that much of a difference to her. Now that the matter's been resolved, I can tell her the truth."

"Damn it, Kramer. I could fire you for this."

"Somehow, I knew you'd remember to point that out sometime during this conversation. You know, Max, you're allowing yourself to become quite predictable at times."

Max was silent.

"How's Dr. Feldman?" Joel asked after a moment.

"Elated. He's already begging for the return of his assistant."

"We can talk about this when I get back. I'll make the arrangements to return today."

"You do that."

Joel heard the click of the receiver. He slowly replaced the phone on its hook.

The waiter returned with his coffee. Joel thanked him and took the cup out on the deck overlooking the harbor.

So it was over... Their idyllic time together was at an end. How ironic that Max had waited until today to call. Twenty-four hours earlier and Joel could have told Melissa before the ceremony. But then, maybe it was better this way. She might be upset with him at first. After all, they *had* met under false pretenses. But all of that had changed so quickly. Their friendship had grown, creating strong bonds between them.

He finished the coffee and went back inside the restaurant, paid the waiter and drove back to the cottage.

He let himself in quietly and listened, but could not hear her stirring. When he walked down the hallway to the bedroom, he found that Melissa still slept. Her tumbled hair framed her face. The light covering draped across her body, revealing no more than her arms and shoulders, but it didn't matter. Joel had a very good memory and had spent the previous night learning all the contours of that body.

He walked into the bathroom and shut the door. Stripping off his clothes, he turned on the shower and stepped beneath the spray, adjusting the temperature.

Memories of the night before came back to him and he couldn't restrain the smile that appeared on his face.

God, but she was one beautiful lady. She'd been so shy with him at first. But later, she had responded so ardently, without shame and with a trust that humbled him.

He'd never received a more beautiful gift in his life.

By the time Joel stepped out of the shower, he felt ready to face the world. He and Melissa were married. No one, including Max, could do anything about that. He would take her back to Virginia so that she could work with Feldman once again.

If she became upset because he hadn't told her the truth about his occupation he would just remind her that if it hadn't been for this job, they would never have met. Surely she would understand the necessity of what he had done.

When he came out of the bathroom, he went over to the bed and crawled in beside her. She stirred, moving against him. He leaned over and kissed her.

"Melissa?"

"Mmm?"

"Are you awake?"

"Uh-uh."

"Are you ready to go home?"

She opened her eyes. "Today?"

"If you want."

"But I thought we were going to have a honeymoon here?"

"There was a call from the States this morning. They're ready for you to come back to work."

She groaned. "Wouldn't you know it? What timing!"

"That doesn't mean the honeymoon has to be over, does it?"

She smiled sleepily. "I don't suppose so." She ran her hand across his chest. "Mmmmm. You feel so good."

"I was thinking the very same thing about you." He gathered her into his arms and began to kiss her. Max could wait. Feldman could wait. The whole world could wait. Nothing was more important to Joel than the woman he held in his arms.

The next time Joel awoke, it was after one o'clock. He glanced at the bed beside him and realized he was alone. There was a crash in the kitchen and he sat up. Was that what had awakened him?

"Melissa?"

There was another sound, like glass shattering. What was happening? Why didn't she answer him?

He grabbed his pants and slid his feet into sandals. From the sound of things, there was likely to be glass all over the floor.

When he walked into the kitchen, Joel froze. Melissa had broken a glass all right. She'd obviously been surprised by the man who now held her with his arm around her throat, a knife in his other hand.

"So we meet again, amigo," the man said, watching Joel. His heart sank. How in the hell had Benito Ortiz found him here? For that matter, how did the man know his first attempt at killing him hadn't been successful?

In the year since Joel had left Central America, he'd taken Max's advice about this man. Max had promised him that other operatives would get him, and Joel had believed him. Obviously, Max had been wrong. Max didn't like being proved wrong. It made him downright cranky, but no more so than Joel felt at the moment.

"What do you want, Ortiz?"

The man smiled, revealing a gold tooth. "Is that any way to greet a friend?"

"When the so-called friend is holding my wife at knife point, it is."

"*Esposa?*" Ortiz began to laugh. "I had no idea you were married, amigo. She probably wasn't too pleased with your condition after the last time we met."

"She doesn't know about that."

"Oh. Secrets. I like that. She doesn't need to know everything."

"That's always been my philosophy," Joel replied absently, trying to make eye contact with Melissa in an effort to reassure her. However, her wide-eyed gaze carried too much fear to receive any silent message he tried to send her.

"Let her go, Ortiz."

"But I have come such a long way to find you, amigo. I like having your full attention when we speak."

"What do you want with me?"

"For one thing, I want to know how you managed to survive the blast that destroyed your apartment."

Melissa blinked and stared at Joel.

"My apartment?"

"Apartment 5A, right?"

"Wrong. My apartment was 5B."

"Ah. I see. Then I was misinformed. You were spotted in apartment 5A the night before."

"By whom?"

"Does it matter? Someone was paid to watch you."

"Watch me or my wife?"

Ortiz glanced at the woman he held. "I never knew she existed. Why would I have her watched?"

"You mean you've been tailing me?"

"But of course. How else would I have found you here? You are good, but you are not infallible, my friend."

Joel forced himself to concentrate on the moment. He would think about all of the ramifications of what he'd just heard later.

"Well, now you've found me. What do you want?"

"You have some information I need. I wasn't aware of who you are until after I tried to kill you last year."

Joel watched Melissa react to that information.

"What sort of information?"

"Who you report to. How many of you are working in our country. Who in our country is providing help."

"And, of course, if I give you all that information," Joel said, slowly but steadily moving toward Melissa and Ortiz, "you'll let us both go, right?"

"I have no quarrel with your wife. Only with you, amigo."

Joel continued to speak softly and soothingly as he edged toward them. "Well, you don't give me much choice now, do you. There's no reason to include my wife in our discussion, so if you—"

Joel made his move. The knife careened out of Ortiz's hand, and Ortiz released his hold on Melissa, already unconscious from the blow to the side of his head made by Joel's foot. By the time Ortiz hit the floor, Joel had scooped up the knife and grabbed Melissa.

"Are you all right?"

She stared at him as though she'd never seen him before. "Who are you?" she whispered hoarsely.

"Your husband, for one thing." He let go of her, then stepped over Ortiz's inert body. "I'll be right back. I've got to find something to keep him immobile until I can get to a phone."

His mind was racing with all of the information that he had just learned. He had to get some help. He couldn't handle this one alone.

When he came back into the kitchen with a length of rope, he found Melissa sitting in one of the chairs, staring at Ortiz. She didn't look up.

"I'm sorrier than I can say that this happened, love. I'm going to have to take him to the village so that I can make a phone call. Do you want to come with me?"

She shook her head without looking at him.

He wasted no time tying the unconscious man so that he couldn't move. Then he walked over to Melissa and knelt beside her chair. He took her hands, which she held clenched between her knees, and rubbed them. They were icy. "I've got to go. Are you sure you'll be all right here?"

She nodded.

"I'll get back as soon as possible. Then we can talk." He waited, but when she didn't respond, he turned her chin so that she was facing him. "Okay?"

The look in her eyes startled him. He had seen the fear in their depths when Ortiz had been holding her. The fear was gone. Now she stared at him as though he were a stranger... a not completely acceptable stranger.

It was the shock. Nothing like this had ever happened to her before. Of course, she wouldn't know how to deal with it.

Rising to his feet, Joel said, "Look, I've got to go. But you'll be all right until I can get back. Then I'll explain everything. You'll see."

He found a place with a phone on the outskirts of the village. He knew Ortiz wasn't going anywhere, but he didn't want anyone to see the man if he could avoid it.

After getting permission to use the phone, he quickly made connection with Max. As soon as Max answered, Joel reported what had happened, ending with, "So what do you want me to do with him? At the moment, I've got him tied up in the back seat of the car."

"Let me make some phone calls. I have some contacts in that area who should be able to help us out on this one. Tell me where you'll be."

Thank God he'd studied the island. Joel recalled an abandoned house on a solitary stretch of road where they could meet without being observed. He gave Max the directions.

As soon as he had finished, Max said, "I'll have someone pick him up shortly. How's Melissa taking all this?"

"Not too well, I'm afraid."

"Not surprising. I want you two out of there as soon as possible. Then I want you to report to me. Maybe we can turn this situation to our advantage."

"I thought you promised me that this guy would be taken care of."

"I thought he was. A positive ID was made on a body."

"Obviously someone was mistaken."

"Joel, these things happen."

"Yeah, I know. It's a rotten business."

"Maybe so. But where would we be without people willing to do what we're doing?"

"At this point, I don't know and I don't care. My wife of all of twelve hours was held at knife point. She could have been killed. As far as I'm concerned, nothing is worth that kind of risk."

"I understand, Kramer. I really do. Come on back and we'll talk about it, okay?"

"Sure. I just don't think that talking is going to change anything. I can't let anything like this happen again."

He hung up and went back to the car. Ortiz hadn't moved. If he was conscious, he wasn't giving anything away. Joel didn't care. He almost wished the guy would try something.

It was more than an hour before he returned to the cottage. Melissa was not in any of the rooms. As he searched through the house, he panicked, wondering if Ortiz had been working with a second man. Damn it! Where could she be?

He glanced out the window and spotted her walking along the beach. She was a small, solitary figure in the distance.

His heart twisted in his chest. He loped down to the beach and began to jog to where she was. When he finally got close enough, he called out to her.

"Melissa?"

She stopped walking and turned around, facing him.

He took her by the shoulders. "It's okay, love. Everything's taken care of. You're safe now. Surely you know I'd never let anything or anyone hurt you. Haven't I always promised you that?"

She looked up at him, her expression calm, her eyes showing nothing but faint curiosity.

"You aren't a writer, are you?"

Whatever he'd expected her to say to him, that wasn't it. He'd planned to give her the explanations about his cover later, after he'd told her about Ortiz and why he was after him. But it didn't really matter. All of it had to be discussed sometime.

He dropped his hold on one of her shoulders and guided her into some shade. Motioning for her to sit down, he sank down beside her. "No. I'm not a writer."

Her next question came at him like a blow to the ribs, effectively knocking the breath from him. "You're a killer, aren't you?"

He stared at her in shock. When he could get his breath, he asked, "Why would you think that?"

"I watched you when you saw that horrible man. You weren't afraid of him at all. I could tell."

He shook his head. "You're wrong. I was petrified when I saw him holding that knife on you."

She gave her head a small negative shake. "No. You knew you could get it away from him."

He thought about that for a moment. "Perhaps," he conceded. "But I wasn't certain that he wouldn't hurt you first."

She met his gaze with a level one of her own. "There was never a doubt in your mind that you had the upper hand. You're a professional and it showed."

Joel didn't know what to say except to reiterate, "I'm no killer."

There was so much to explain that he didn't know where to start. He was searching for the right words when she asked, "Who do you work for?"

That was easy enough to answer. "I work for the government."

"You mean *our* government?" she asked suspiciously.

Joel could feel anger begin to work through his body. He forced himself to take several deep, calming breaths before he answered. "Yes. I work for the United States government."

"How come you moved across the hall from me?"

That question reminded him of what Ortiz had said. "You were right. That bomb was meant for me." He shook his head, still amazed at the turn of events."

"I knew it wasn't meant for me," she pointed out with irritation.

"Melissa. I haven't been cleared to tell you this, but I'm going to anyway." She waited. "Peter Feldman was almost killed in a car accident about a month ago."

She stared at him in shocked disbelief. "Dr. Feldman? How badly was he hurt? Why didn't someone tell me?" Then she looked at Joel suspiciously. "How do you know?"

He tried to answer her questions in order. "Besides bruises and contusions, he fractured his leg. He preferred not to upset you. But he wanted you to be protected. So he contacted my boss."

"Your boss?" she repeated in a careful voice.

"He just wanted you safe."

"You mean, you were hired to watch out for me?"

He nodded.

"So all this time when I thought I was making friends with you, you were just doing the job you were hired to do?"

"Of course not! There was a possibility that you needed some protection, but no one was really sure of that. I was between assignments with nothing to do. So I agreed to move in across the hall in case any trouble developed." All the time he was explaining, she watched him politely. He had no idea whether or not she was accepting what he was saying. "Once we met, everything changed. You know what happened. You were there. We spent time together—"

"That was part of your job," she pointed out.

"Partly, yes, it was. But there was so much more happening between us!" He ran his hand through his hair. "Damn! This wasn't the way I wanted to tell you. It wasn't the way you're trying to make it sound and you know it."

"Do I?" She studied him in silence for a few moments. "All right. Perhaps you should tell me how it was."

"The more I was around you, the more I learned about you, the more I enjoyed your company. We became friends. I hadn't realized how lonely my life was until you came into it and filled in all the blank spaces. By the time we came down here—"

"What would you have done if Karen hadn't allowed us to come down here?"

He shrugged. "We could have found a place somewhere safe. But you have to admit this was perfect."

She nodded. "I played right into your hands, didn't I?" She looked away, out toward the water. In a low voice, she said, "I made it so easy for you. Green as grass, too naive to be believed. I actually convinced myself that I had suddenly learned social graces, that I could entertain and please a man, that I could make friends easily and enjoy the bantering that friends share." She looked down at her hands. "And all the time, you were being paid to be my companion." She glanced up. "You're nothing more than a glorified baby-sitter."

"Melissa! It isn't like that. Not at all."

She stood. "But now the game is over, or at least my part is. You said my office is being reopened, so I can go back to work."

He came to his feet and stuck his hands in his pockets. "It's more than that. They caught the two men who were responsible for Dr. Feldman's accident. They didn't want him to finish the research he'd been doing."

She jerked her head around to look at him. "No one knows what he's been researching. Not even me."

"Somebody found out. He was afraid that whoever it was would think that you also knew what he was doing. He was afraid for you, but he didn't want you to be upset."

She started walking back toward the house. "And he didn't trust me enough to tell me about it."

"It wasn't a matter of trust, can't you see that? We just wanted to keep you safe."

She repeated the word *safe* beneath her breath as though it were an obscenity.

They were almost to the house when she said, "You didn't need to marry me, you know," in a conversational tone. "I would have made love to you at anytime. All you would have had to do was to let me know that you wanted me."

He stopped her, his hand on her arm. "Please stop this, Melissa. Please. Nothing has really changed between us. We are the same two people who spoke their vows together just twenty-four hours ago."

"Is that what you think, that nothing has changed? How can you possibly look me straight in the eye and say that? *Everything* has changed. Don't you understand? Our relationship was built on lies. You are nothing like the man I thought I married." She turned away for a moment and brushed her hand across her eyes. When she turned back, he could still see the sheen of tears.

She gave a small, broken laugh. "You know, it's really funny when you think about it. I'd never realized how hopelessly naive I am . . . how gullible. I saw you as shy and a little unsure of yourself with women. I was touched by that shyness, and I found myself reaching out to you, to reassure you." She shook her head. "Isn't that a riot? You're an agent for the government, and I thought you were shy? I bet you were laughing your head off about that."

She spun away and climbed the steps to the house. She walked along the porch to the door of her bedroom.

He followed her. "Melissa, there isn't a man anywhere who doesn't feel a sense of unsureness, a sense of shyness, when he meets a woman who affects him the way you immediately did me. I didn't know what had hit me. Sure, it bothered me that I was assigned to watch out for you once I realized I was falling in love with you. That's why I tried to keep my distance from you as much as possible." He threw his arms wide in exasperation. "Unfortunately, I couldn't keep my damn hands off you. I at least had to be able to hold you, to kiss you, to express the way I feel for you. I think I could have handled that all right if I hadn't learned that you loved me."

She paled beneath her tan. "What are you talking about?"

"The night you were bitten by the snake. You were delirious and were talking to someone about me."

"And I said that I loved you?"

"Yes."

"So you figured that if I was in love with you, I'd probably marry you."

"I hoped you would. Yes. The snake bite brought home how devastated I would be if I were to lose you. I didn't want to take any chances. I knew I loved you. When I found out that you felt the same way, I knew we could work out any problems together."

She shook her head. "You forgot one small detail."

"What's that?"

"Our relationship was built on lies. You are nothing like the man I thought I married. You are a liar. Your whole life is a lie. How can you possibly expect me to believe anything you say to me?"

The series of emotional body punches he'd taken were making themselves felt. He had no more explanations. He had no more arguments. When he stood there in silence watching her, she went on.

"Perhaps marrying me appeased your conscience. I don't know. I'll probably never know. All I know is that I want to go home, I want to return to work, and I never want to have anything to do with you again."

She turned away from him and went into her room, closing the door behind her.

## Chapter Eleven

A warm tropical breeze wafted over his sensitive body as he lay near the turquoise-blue water. He sighed. The scents of the island were all around him, and he could feel the sun's rays caressing him.

He felt her touch as she brushed her fingertips across his chest. Without opening his eyes, he smiled, pleased that she had decided to join him once again. He caught the delicate scent of her floral perfume and his heart increased its rhythm and became a throbbing drumbeat within him.

She touched his nipple with the tip of her tongue, causing the expected reaction. He slid his hand into her hair and lifted her face to his until their lips met.

She felt so good in his arms, so damned good. He rolled, placing her delectable form beneath him. Their kiss deepened, and their tongues joined in a playful duel. He continued to caress her silken skin . . . exploring, loving, delighting in her. She was his, would always be his.

He loved her so much. He couldn't imagine life without her, couldn't imagine—

She disappeared, suddenly and without a trace, like an early-morning mist dissipates when touched by the sun. His arms no longer held her. She was gone and there was nothing he could do, nothing he could do, nothing—

Joel jerked awake and pushed himself up on one elbow. The digital clock beside his bed read 4:09.

Damn. It was too early to get up, which meant that he would have to lie there and wait for dawn. Wait and think, because he sure as hell wasn't going back to sleep.

In the three months since he'd last seen Melissa, he'd dreamed about her every damn night. Would those dreams never end?

He'd spent one night with her—one incredible night that continued to haunt him. His subconscious mind had insisted on replaying the events for him like a popular rerun on television. The settings sometimes changed, but the content of the dream remained the same.

He'd tried several remedies to break the pattern, from working until he fell asleep exhausted to a couple of evenings spent with a bottle of bourbon. But nothing helped.

Melissa haunted him, waking or sleeping.

He folded his arms beneath his head and stared up at the shadowy ceiling. His mind slipped into the familiar groove of remembering their last day together.

He'd understood her anger, at least to a degree. He found it hard to believe that she couldn't see, couldn't believe how much he loved her, but he figured that being as intelligent as she was, she would calm down if he would give her some time.

He'd gone to his room and packed, told the woman he'd hired to keep the food that was still in the house, and when Melissa came out of the bedroom with her bag, he had placed their luggage in the car. Neither of them spoke.

They'd gotten a boat ride to one of the larger islands and booked a flight to Miami. Joel attempted conversation with Melissa during the trip, but she had either answered his questions with a minimum of words or did not comment when he spoke.

He'd never seen her like that before, so closed. It was as though she had withdrawn from her body, leaving a shell that functioned on autopilot.

When they arrived in Miami, he went to make arrangements for their flight to D.C. Then he returned to where he'd left her sitting to find she was gone. So was her bag. She'd left his bag beside the empty chair.

Joel spent the next two hours looking for her, having her paged, watching every departing plane's line of passengers as they boarded.

She had just disappeared.

Even after he returned to D.C., he searched for her. It was more difficult to know where to begin since she didn't have a home. After spending the necessary time with Max to hear the details of the case, he went back to his apartment. There had been no place else for him to go.

He'd waited until the following morning and called her office. He'd asked for her, but when the phone was answered, a male voice spoke.

"Feldman."

"Good morning, Doctor. This is Joel Kramer. I understand you're going to have a complete recovery from your accident. I was pleased to hear the news."

"Joel! Thank God you called. I'd almost decided that you had permanently kidnapped my invaluable assistant. Are you two still on the island?"

The dull pain in Joel's chest, the one that he'd carried with him since her disappearance, increased.

"I'm in Virginia. I'd hoped that Melissa had returned to work. That's why I called—to speak with her."

"You mean you don't know where she is?"

"I'm afraid not."

"But you were supposed to be looking after her!" Joel could still remember the anger in Feldman's voice.

"I did my best. Once she realized that I had been her assigned protector, she became quite upset. She vanished soon after we arrived in Miami."

"I see."

"Look, Doctor, I would really appreciate your taking my phone number and address and giving it to her when she calls or shows up there. We need to talk."

She never called. He waited a week before he gave in to the gnawing desire to hear something and called the lab once again. During that second call, Dr. Feldman explained that he had given Melissa Joel's message when she called in. He'd been concerned because she had called to explain that she would not be returning and asked that her check and any personal items left at her desk be mailed to an address in New York.

Joel eventually had tracked down Karen's phone number in New York. Another dead end. Karen was polite, but insisted she hadn't talked with Melissa since she'd returned from the island. She asked about their stay, accepted his thanks for their time there and took his phone number and address to give to Melissa as soon as she got in touch with her.

In the three months since then, he'd periodically called both people to see if they had heard from Melissa. Both insisted they had not.

He'd run into a brick wall. He'd lost his wife and didn't know how the hell he was going to find her. He'd finally broken down and asked Max to help. Like it or not, he knew that Max could find out if she was working anywhere in the United States. If she had a job, she would have used her social-security number, she'd have a bank account, she'd be using charge cards.

Max found where she banked. She'd withdrawn all her savings and closed her checking account and had quite effectively disappeared.

How long could she last without working? Surely she'd have to surface somewhere.

Max had promised to keep a watch for her and had insisted on sending Joel on his proposed assignment. He had pointed out that Joel wasn't accomplishing a great deal while he paced up and down his apartment.

Joel had been back in the States a week now. Max had nothing new to report.

How could she just walk away? How could she pretend that their marriage had never happened? Joel had gotten a copy of the recorded marriage license and kept it lying beside his bed as a reminder that he hadn't dreamed the whole scenario.

He didn't even have a picture of her. He had nothing but memories. And dreams.

Sometimes, he had nightmares that Ortiz had somehow managed to escape and had kidnapped her, but Max assured him that Ortiz was locked away in a high-security cell.

Joel finally realized that he could do nothing more. He had to accept the fact that her trust in him had been destroyed. Now all he had to do was to live with that knowledge, to stop replaying all the possible ways he could have handled the situation with the hope of a more positive outcome.

He sat on the side of the bed and rubbed his jaw. He hadn't shaved the day before and his chin felt rough. He grabbed a pair of jogging shorts and drew them on, then went into the kitchen and put on the coffee. While it was brewing, he slipped on his sneakers and went down to the corner for the Sunday paper.

When he returned, the coffee was ready. He poured himself a cup and went into the living room, opening the paper. He hadn't looked at the headlines until now. Now that he saw them, he wondered how they had failed to catch his attention.

## BREAKTHROUGH IN CONTROLLING AD-DICTIONS ANNOUNCED

Most of the story was on the second page, but it was all there, with extensive quotes from the pharmaceutical company. Dr. Feldman had done it.

There were still months of testing to be done, but the members of the group that had agreed to test the new discovery were enthusiastic with their comments regarding their lack of desire to return to abusive use of addictive substances. The chemical appeared to be working. Only time would tell if the DNA change would be permanent.

Perhaps the company and the government felt that the best protection under the circumstances was a barrage of publicity. The public was being made aware. There would be no chance now to stop the progress Dr. Feldman was making.

Joel turned a few pages before another piece of the paper fell out . . . the Sunday-supplement magazine. On the front cover were the words, "Can You Tell Your Future by the Stars?"

Joel no longer felt the anger that had swept over him when he'd first read the description of a man born between May 21 and June 20. He'd had time to think about the comments and had come to terms with most of them. Perhaps he did have a dual personality. Perhaps he did prefer change to routine.

But the article had been wrong about willingness to commit himself to a stable relationship. In his case, both aspects of his personality were deeply in love with Dr. Melissa Jordan. He would be willing to give up his double existence, to find a desk job somewhere in order to establish a home with her.

Not that his wishes or desires seemed to matter. He threw down the paper. He'd go get a shower, clean up a little. He rubbed his jaw once more. Might even shave. Then he'd get out of the house for a while. He was sick of his own company, but not ready to go on another assignment. At least he was in the same country with her, or so he assumed. There weren't too many countries she could visit without some kind of identification.

As far as Max could tell, she'd made no applications for a replacement of the documents that were in her purse at the time of the explosion. It was as though she was determined to be a nonperson.

He turned on the shower, then decided to shave first. He was halfway finished when he thought he heard the phone. He opened the bathroom door and listened. Sure enough, the shrill sound rang out clearly. But by the time he reached the phone, it was no longer ringing. He picked it up anyway, but wasn't surprised to hear the dial tone.

Joel punched in the numbers for the only person who would be calling him. As soon as Max answered, Joel asked, "Did you just call me?"

"You already restless?"

"No! My phone was ringing, but by the time I got to it, you'd already hung up."

"It wasn't me, Kramer. I've got better things to do."

Joel thought for a moment, then shrugged. "Probably a wrong number."

"It could be your adoring public."

"Go to hell," Joel grumbled and hung up on the sound of Max's laughter.

He returned to the shower and stepped under the soothing spray. Maybe he'd go out for a late breakfast. He missed having people around. He'd discovered something surprising on this last assignment. Work could be boring, no matter how potentially dangerous. The island vacation had been an eye-opener to him in many ways. He had learned to relax, to enjoy a leisurely schedule.

He'd liked it.

The water had cooled considerably by the time he stepped out of the shower. He'd enjoyed the refreshing feel of it. Even though it was still morning, the day had turned out hot, which was typical for this time of year.

He heard the doorbell while he was still drying the moisture from his dripping body.

"What the hell—"

He strode out of the bathroom, clutching the towel around his waist. If kids were ringing his doorbell, he was going to put a stop to it right now. He jerked the door open, saying, "Now, listen here—" Then forgot what he was going to say.

Melissa stood there before him, looking cool in a sleeveless dress made of a thin material with swirls of color that blended beautifully with her eyes. Sandals with heels put her at eye level with him.

"I'm sorry, I seem to have caught you at a bad time."

"Melissa!" Over the months, he had fantasized all the different ways they would meet again, but in each one, he had envisioned himself as catching her unawares . . . not the other way around.

His hair was dripping water down his face, but he couldn't use his towel without exposing himself. He motioned her inside. "Hang on a moment and I'll get dressed. I won't be but a second. Uh, have a seat and, uh, help yourself to the coffee."

Joel beat a hasty retreat to the bedroom where he grabbed the first thing he saw to wear, his jogging shorts. As soon as he had them on, he quickly began to towel dry his hair and moved toward the living room once more.

"I can't believe that . . ." He paused, looking around. She was nowhere in sight. He started toward the front door when he heard the slight clink of china from the kitchen. Joel managed to release the air that he seemed to have been holding in his lungs since he'd first opened the door and found her standing there.

He paused in the kitchen doorway, his hands resting lightly on his hips, and watched her pour coffee into a cup, her back to him. He began to notice things that he'd been too surprised at first to take note of. She was much thinner than she'd been. Her waist looked small enough for him to circle with his hands.

She'd cut her hair. It curled softly around the nape of her neck and around her ears. She'd lost her tan, which was surprising, since the weather had been warm for several weeks now.

"Where have you been?"

He hadn't realized he was going to ask until he heard the words.

She spun around with a gasp. When she saw him standing there, she held her hand to her throat. "You scared me."

"Did it ever occur to you that your disappearing act might have scared me? I had no way of knowing if one of Ortiz's men had grabbed you when my back was turned."

She turned away from Joel and picked up her cup. Without looking at him again, she walked over to the small table and sat down. "I never thought of that," she said, looking down at her coffee. She glanced up. "Did you get in trouble for not protecting me sufficiently?"

He stalked over and dropped into the chair across from her. "What the hell kind of question is that? I've been worried out of my mind about you. I've called everybody I knew who could possibly have heard from you. I've checked every lead I could think of, wondering where you were, how you were surviving—" He stopped for a moment, then ran his hand through his hair. "I don't understand any of this. Why did you quit your job? Why did you just walk away? Why did you decide to come see me now?"

She toyed with the handle of her cup. "I tried to call first. When there was no answer, I thought you might be out of town, so I decided to come over and put a note in your mailbox. The manager saw me looking at the boxes. I explained that I was looking for you, and he said he thought he'd seen you earlier, coming in with a paper." She tucked a curl behind her ear. "So I decided to come up to see if you'd gotten back."

He leaned back in his chair. "So you found me. I have a hunch it was a little easier for you than what I've been going through."

He watched soft color pinken her face. "Yes. Karen and Dr. Feldman both gave me your messages."

"And you immediately rushed out and called me, right?"

She raised her head and looked at him, her color still high. "I've never seen you like this before—at least, not until that last day when that man was there."

"Oh, yeah. I remember. You were upset because I wasn't the pleasant, shy, introverted writer you'd decided I was."

"That was who you were pretending to be."

"I wasn't pretending anything with you, Melissa. I was always who I am, all except for my occupation, which I was specifically instructed not to tell you. Everything I told you about my past was true. I hid nothing from you."

"But you are shaped by the job you do, Joel. Everybody is."

"I'm not arguing that. But I'm not a liar. And I'm certainly not a killer, as you so quickly decided." He could no longer sit still. He pushed the chair back, got up and stalked to the window in the living room.

"I know that," she said in a low voice.

"When did you change your mind?" he asked without looking around.

She got up and wandered over to the sofa. When she sat down, she leaned her head wearily against the back. "I don't even remember. I just remember being so confused." She was quiet for several minutes, but he didn't interrupt the silence that was forming around them.

Joel prayed that she wouldn't see the tremor that had taken over his body as soon as he first saw her. It was as though he'd been plugged into an electrical current that was sending a steady charge through him, causing a visible vibration. He'd received many shocks in his life, some nasty ones that other men had been unable to withstand with his composure, but nothing that had ever happened to him had shaken him so much as seeing Melissa so unexpectedly again.

"I was lying in bed a few weeks ago and I finally figured out an analogy of how I felt that last day I was with you."

Her voice was low and a little hoarse, as though she was having trouble getting the words out. Joel slowly turned away from the window and faced her. He didn't speak.

"From the time I met you, my life became magical. The only problem was, I thought it was all real. I got caught up in the magic and the emotions. Because I'd never had a close relationship with a man before, I projected every male role I'd ever conceived onto you. You were the loving, affectionate father I'd never had, the teasing older brother, the flirting boy next door, my first date, my first romance, my first love. You became Sir Lancelot and Sir Galahad all rolled up into one, as well as all the princes in all the fairy tales to me. And because you said you loved me, I became the beautiful princess—with charm and confidence and elegance—all the things I never have been."

He stared at her in amazement at her assessment of herself, but still he didn't say anything.

"I was caught up in all the make believe, and then that horrible man showed up and suddenly, I felt as though the lights were turned on all around me and the curtains were drawn. The play was over and the audience had all gone home. All except for me. I'd gotten so caught up in the story, I hadn't realized that none of it was real. I was still sitting there, waiting for the play to go on and on. But you were no longer willing to play the part. Your lines were through. It was time to return home for a new role."

She had closed her eyes rather than look at him, but that had not prevented the tears from sliding down her cheeks. She looked so vulnerable, and he loved her so much.

Joel sat beside her on the sofa. She opened her eyes and looked at him. "So I blamed you rather than face the fact that all the fantasies and fairy tales had been in my head. Meeting you caused me to realize how much I've missed in my life—fun times with friends, tender times, passionate times. I skipped from child prodigy to adulthood without the learning times that go with being an adolescent. You coaxed the adolescent in me to come out and play." The smile she gave him was genuine, even though the tears continued to slip down her cheeks. "I came here today because I wanted you to know that I'm sorry for blaming you for bringing me out of my beautiful little bubble. You taught me so much about myself, things that I could never have learned on my own." She touched his hand ever so gently. "I came to thank you for everything you did . . . for taking such good care of me, even when I didn't know that was what you were doing . . . for being a friend so that I could understand what friendship means . . . for teaching me about love . . . for giving me the gifts of understanding, and tolerance, and compassion."

He turned his hand so that he could clasp hers. "Melissa?"

"Yes?"

"Why do you think I married you?"

She smiled. "But you didn't, Joel. I realized that later. You just wanted me to feel better about making love to you. But it really wasn't necessary. I was never so naive as to think a man of your experience would allow himself to be legally tied to someone."

"A good point and one I'm pleased that you can appreciate. I *am* experienced in the world. No one can force me to do something that I don't want to do." He released her hand and stood. "I'll be back in a moment."

Joel went into the bedroom and came out holding a folded piece of paper that he handed to her. He watched as she slowly opened it and even more slowly read what it said. He noticed that she recognized her own signature…and his…as well as that of the minister who had married them.

She looked up at him, puzzled and obviously shaken. "But this—this says the original of this document has been recorded—as though this is officially a— That you and I are actually—" She seemed to run out of words.

"So you thought I lied about this, as well," he said, the pain of that knowledge going through him like a sword.

"After I calmed down and really thought about everything that happened, it didn't make any logical sense for you to have taken our relationship to that extreme."

"Well, Dr. Jordan, you overlooked an obvious equation."

She gave him a questioning look.

"There was only one reason why I would marry you. I told you at the time and I did not lie." Joel felt as though a hand suddenly seized him by the throat so that he could not say another word without choking. He swallowed a couple of times and cleared his throat. In a gruff voice, he managed to say, "I love you, Melissa. That was never a fantasy. I'm no knight in shining armor. I'm sure as hell no prince, but I fell in love with you so hard, the crash was probably heard for miles around. I knew that marrying you without telling you why we were together was unethical. I came close to losing my job over it, but at the time, I didn't care. I loved you and I truly believed that you loved me. No matter what else I am, what else I've ever done, I would never say the vows that I repeated to you unless they came from my heart."

It was only when she brushed her thumb across his cheekbone that he became aware of the moisture there.

"Oh, Joel," she whispered. "What have I done?"

He saw his pain reflected in her face and he knew that she had been suffering these past three months as much as he had. He slid his arms around her and drew her close. "You've come home, Melissa...where you belong."

## Chapter Twelve

Joel discovered that memories paled by comparison to having Melissa there in his arms. She had thrown her arms around his neck and held him so tightly, he could scarcely breathe. He scooped her into his arms and carried her down the hallway to his bedroom.

The bed covers looked as though a battle had been fought with them without a winner. He shoved them aside as he lowered her onto his bed. Her dress was surprisingly easy to remove. Her slip quickly followed. He skimmed her hose and shoes from her as though by magic.

"You've lost weight," he whispered, touching his lips to her breast, her waist, her abdomen.

"So have you."

"Wonder if it could be for the same reason?" He nudged her legs apart so that he could place a trail of kisses along her inner thigh.

"Oh, Joel, I've been so stupid," she said with a quick, sobbing breath.

"You won't get any argument out of me on that one." He leaned forward and first kissed her mouth, traced her lips with his tongue, then nibbled on her bottom lip.

When she opened her mouth to him, all conversation ceased.

Several hours later, the bed covers were on the floor. Joel and Melissa were still intertwined on the bed. He had both arms around her; she had her head on his chest and one of his thighs was sandwiched between both of hers.

"Was that your stomach or mine?" she murmured drowsily.

"Probably both, in perfect harmony."

They continued to lay there, each touching the other from time to time, as though to make sure they were not dreaming.

Finally, he sighed and said, "You never did answer me."

"About what?"

"Where you've been."

"Oh. I'm not that sure. Once I left the airport in Miami, I realized I had no place to go and very little money. I caught a shuttle bus into town, then called my bank to find out how to transfer money. I had a terrible time trying to prove who I was after it was sent."

"I had nightmares of you lost somewhere, cold and hungry, with no money and no way to know how to contact me. I'd wake up in a cold sweat."

"I could have contacted Karen for help if I'd gotten desperate. I just needed time to think. Once I got my money, I went to the bus station and took the first bus north, then transferred to one going west. I ended up near the Gulf somewhere in Mississippi, found an inexpensive bed-and-breakfast place and spent most of my time walking up and down the beach.''

"Then why are you so pale?"

She touched his chest with her fingers and he shivered. He grabbed them and held them firmly against him. "No fair. You're trying to distract me."

"How am I doing?"

"I want to know what happened to that fabulous tan you had, especially if you've been spending your time on the beach."

She sighed. "I got sick. I wasn't eating right. I couldn't sleep. I felt as though I was in a nightmare that I couldn't escape."

"I know the feeling," he muttered.

"One morning, I just couldn't force myself out of bed. My landlady came in to check on me later that day and said I was running a high temperature. I was really ill for quite a while."

"But, of course, you wouldn't call me."

"I was in no condition to talk with anyone."

"You could have given the number to your landlady."

She shook her head. "I was too ashamed of the way I'd behaved by that time."

"Has anyone ever pointed out to you just how tough you are on yourself? Cut yourself a little slack, sweetheart. It's all right to be human. And none of us are perfect." He ran his hand along her waist, over her hips and down her thigh. "You come damn close, though."

"I never told you that I loved you, not in all the time we were together. That's why I was so shocked to learn that you knew."

"Was there a particular reason you didn't want me to know?"

"I didn't want to embarrass you or make you feel obligated to me in some way."

"Are you certain that you actually earned all those degrees, lady? It's hard for me to fathom that someone with your vast knowledge could be so incredibly unlearned."

"But I am. At least, about love."

He hugged her to him. "I have a confession to make. I haven't been a real scholar on the subject, myself. But it's amazing how quickly a person can learn when he gets involved."

"But it's something that we have to experience to understand, isn't it?"

He kissed the crown of her head, all that he could see at the moment. "I suppose it is," he agreed.

"So, what are we going to do now?"

"Eat?" he asked hopefully.

"I mean about our marriage."

He pulled away so that he could see her face. "If you think you're going to get away from me again, then you're—"

"I just mean, are we going to live here? Or is this a temporary place for you?"

"It's the only home I have, but that doesn't mean we can't look around for something larger, or a house, maybe. Whatever you want."

"I was thinking about contacting Dr. Feldman tomorrow."

"I have a feeling he'd be delighted. We've become acquainted over the months you've been gone. He's been quite concerned about you."

"Does he know we're married?"

"I didn't think it was my place to tell him."

"Does Max know?"

"You bet. How do you think I almost got fired?"

"How about your job?"

"What do you mean?"

"Are you going to be watching over damsels in distress much?"

He grinned. "I don't know. Do you think I have an aptitude for the job? Should I find me a coat of shining armor?" He gave a slight grunt when she poked him in the ribs.

"Your work seems to be very dangerous."

"Not ordinarily, but it does have its moments."

She was quiet for several minutes. "I would rather have you safe, but I want you to be happy, whatever you do."

"Then you're in luck, doll. I am extremely happy, thanks to you. Now that I know where you are, I can get on with all the plans I wanted to discuss with you before we were so rudely interrupted by Ortiz."

"What plans?"

He began to kiss her. "I'm sure in a few months, when you aren't quite as much of a distraction, they'll come back to me."

"But in the meantime?"

"I'm willing to live our lives one day at a time. How about you?" His second kiss made her forget the subject of their conversation.

"Whatever you say, Joel," she murmured, wrapping her arms around him.

Joel leaned over her, content with his new role. Happy ever after sounded downright exciting to him.

# *Epilogue*

Joel tossed the piece of paper he'd been reading down on the desk and stood up, then stretched. Damn, he must be getting old. After a few hours of sitting, he grew stiff. What he needed was a good workout.

He wandered over to the window of his study and gazed out across the Virginia countryside. They'd been lucky to find a place within commuting distance for Melissa that gave them the acreage and privacy they wanted. The rolling hills beckoned him to saddle one of the horses and take a ride. He glanced at his watch. He might invite some company to join him.

A slight scratching sound at the door caused him to turn his head. "Come in."

A pair of large blue eyes surrounded by a tumbled mop of blond curls peeked around the door. He grinned. "Come on in, Lisa."

A dainty five-year-old tiptoed into the room. "Lucy said not to bother you," she whispered. She took another few steps. "Am I bothering you, Daddy?"

He walked over to her and scooped her up into his arms. "What do you suppose would happen to you if you were?"

"Lucy would scold me."

"Can't say that I blame her."

Lisa cocked her head. "Well-l-l, I thought if I pretended to be the dog and just scratched at the door, you wouldn't notice me if you were busy."

"I see."

"Mommy says when you're working, you don't hear anything."

"I think your mommy may be right."

Lisa leaned back in his arms and looked at him. "Do you want to go play?"

He thought about that for a moment. "I might. Then again, I was thinking about going for a ride."

"On Blaze?"

"Umm-hmm."

"Me, too?"

"If you'd like."

"Tony, too?"

Joel walked out into the hallway. "If he wants."

Lisa scrambled out of his arms. "Tony! Daddy said we could go riding with him!" she yelled, racing toward the other end of the house.

Joel wandered into the kitchen where Lucy was working. "Any coffee left?"

The middle-aged woman glanced around with a smile. "I always keep coffee ready for you. Melissa would skin me alive if she thought I wasn't anticipating your every need and wish."

He poured himself a cup and leaned against the counter, watching her. "Lucy, how long have you been with us?"

She looked up, surprised. "A little over eight years now. Don't you remember? I came to work right after Tony was born."

He nodded, smiling. "How could I forget?"

She shook her head. "That was one fella who was determined to stay awake all night and sleep all day. It took all three of us to keep up with him for a while."

Where had the time gone? They'd been married for two years before Tony arrived. By then, they'd found the home they wanted and Joel had discovered a hidden talent within himself that had changed his working habits. He wasn't certain that Max had ever totally forgiven him. He chuckled. The irony of the situation still amused him. After all, Max had only himself to blame since he was the one who had originally suggested the idea.

"Dad!" A tornado in torn jeans and faded shirt came tearing into the kitchen, his eyes glittering with excitement. "Are you going to let me ride Lady?"

"You think you can handle her?"

"Sure I can. Roy's been helping me practice, but he never lets me out of the pasture. Can I really go with you?"

Joel rumpled his son's untidy hair. "You bet!"

"I'll go tell Roy to get the horses ready!" Tony darted out of the room.

Lucy shook her head. "That boy still has more energy than three people combined. I don't know where he gets it."

Joel finished his cup of coffee. "I'd better get my clothes changed before those two take off without me."

He climbed the stairs and walked toward the master bedroom. He paused at an open doorway and peered into the nursery. Two-year-old Christopher slept as hard as he played. He lay crossways in his bed, his covers bunched around him.

Joel shook his head and walked on. Sometimes, it was hard for him to remember a time when Melissa, Tony, Lisa and Christopher had not been a part of his life. They had become his entire world.

The same thought occurred to him several hours later as he lay in bed, holding Melissa.

"It's hard for me to remember a time when I didn't have you and the children. I can't imagine how I managed."

She was curled so that her head was on his shoulder, one leg across his thighs. She ran her hand across the familiar expanse of his chest, never tiring of touching him. "I know what you mean. I feel the same way."

"Would we have believed it if someone, announcing that he or she was from the future, had told us the outcome of my moving in across the hall from you?"

"Did you ever think you'd no longer be working for Max?"

"I don't think I ever gave the idea much thought." He was quiet for several long minutes. "But I know I would have argued if I'd been told that someday, I'd be making a living as a writer!"

"And on the *New York Times* bestseller list at that!"

They both laughed, remembering how all of that had come about. Melissa's accusations that he had lied to her had continued to rankle. After all, all he had lied about was his profession.

For the first eighteen months after their marriage, Joel continued to take assignments and travel, but whenever he could, he started making notes, jotting down ideas, researching whenever possible, and when he was at home, he dug out several of his college textbooks and brushed up on what he had learned years before.

No one was more surprised than Joel when he sold his first manuscript. Then he found an aggressive agent who encouraged him to keep writing the kind of adventure novels that seemed to flow effortlessly from his brain.

Of course, he had to make certain that no accurate intelligence information was used. Not that people would have believed some of the bizarre situations he'd encountered.

"I got a letter from Abe today," he said, suddenly remembering.

"And what does your esteemed agent have to say?"

"I'm being offered an obscene amount of money to produce ten books over the next ten years."

She raised her head. "Joel! That's wonderful. Why didn't you tell me sooner?"

He pulled her head down and gave her a long, leisurely kiss. When he finally raised his head, he murmured, "I forgot. There were too many other exciting things going on."

Melissa recalled her arrival that day. Tony and Lisa were dancing up and down with their news about the ride, Christopher was chattering and showing her the city that he and his daddy had built out of an array of children's construction toys, so proud of himself. Joel had been wearing an identical grin on his face.

She sighed, settling on his shoulder once more. She loved this man to distraction. He'd shown her what love could be, what family life could be. He'd encouraged her to continue her career, convincing her that she could have it all. He'd been right, but only because he'd been will-

ing to be there with the children, to plan his writing
schedule around their schedules, to answer their questions, tend to their hurts, encourage their questions,
nurture them . . . and her.

"I love you," she whispered, realizing once again how
inadequate those words were to express the tremendous
emotion that swept over her whenever she thought of
everything that Joel had managed to bring to her life.

He shifted so that he was facing her, which left her in
a very vulnerable position. She could feel his arousal
pressed against her.

"Care to demonstrate?" he drawled, nibbling on her
ear.

"It would be a pleasure, sir," she whispered just as her
mouth found his.

It was.

# MORE ABOUT
# THE GEMINI MAN

**by Lydia Lee**

It's your fourth date, and you're beginning to think you misunderstood the twinkle you saw in that Gemini man's eyes when he'd first asked you out a few weeks ago. You'd made plans for a Saturday picnic, but it had rained. No matter, your Gemini friend—and you'd already learned about his birth sign and everything else concerning this gregarious gentleman—whisked you off to the Press Club for an informal lunch. You hadn't known he'd moonlighted as a reporter. You thought he was a computer specialist!

Now you've just gotten out of a midnight movie and you've gone to a quaint café. There, you talk about the film until four in the morning. But, hey, isn't this your *fourth* date? This *is* the twentieth century, and he hasn't even gotten to the handholding stage while you're dreaming of happily ever after! Is there something wrong with the man? You sure hope not, but he *is* pretty changeable.

And just when you'd gotten used to him being a reporter and a computer expert, you find out his real dream in life was to sing as a tenor with the Metropolitan Opera. You discovered this goodie when he surprised you with tickets to *Madame Butterfly*.

Afterward, when he *finally* asks you up to his place for a drink, the first thing you see upon entering the house is a grand piano and a set of drums. Why on earth should it surprise you that he can play everything from Chopin to the Rolling Stones?

So what's with this Gemini man, anyway? Deciding on a little investigating, you get out an astrology book and find out that he's ruled by Mercury—the messenger of the Gods AKA the whiz-kid of communication with a finger in every conceivable pie. One book says he's a jack-of-all-trades. He's light, charming and witty. Frequently, he has two careers and needs variety the way the rest of us need air. What does he look for in a woman? Brains. What's his worse fault? He can change his mind on a dime and make perfect sense doing it. It has been known to drive some people crazy.

He is also a silver-tongued wonder. He can be a stunning orator or the kind of glib con man who sells the Brooklyn Bridge to you one day and buys it back at a profit the next. In matters of the heart, these variety-addicted souls have earned a reputation for, shall we say, inconsistency. But if he's mature and you're on your toes, this shouldn't be a problem. Alas, though, he will probably always be a flirt, albeit a charming one.

Gemini's symbol is the twins, and like Pisces, he's dual-bodied, so it's sometimes difficult to tell which twin is in charge. But if you give this Mercury-ruled man enough room to do his quick changes, and if you can keep up with his facile wit, by the time that fifth date rolls around, he might just do more than talk. Even a Gemini needs a break from all his mental aerobics, and what nicer way to unwind then to cozy up to *you!*

So if you're interested in tripping the light fantastic, you might want to check him out. Look for him in such fields as journalism, travel, education, radio and TV. In short, anything with variety, and preferably something in communications. At first, it may seem that communicating is about all this man *can* do. But given time, he'll find some pretty spectacular ways to communicate his feelings to you. And you will never, ever have a dull moment with this man! After all, Rudolph Valentino and Errol Flynn were Geminis, and they certainly knew how to get across their message!

\*     \*     \*     \*     \*

*Famous Gemini Men*

*Arthur Conan Doyle*
*Bob Dylan*
*Frank Lloyd Wright*
*Al Jolson*
*John F. Kennedy*